Old Florida Drayton Island Tales

By Bruce A. Geiger

Copyright 2013 Bruce A. Geiger

Credit this photo: State Archives of Florida, *Florida Memory*, http://floridamemory.com/itemshow/2675

Preface

Drayton Island is in the St. Johns River system, about one hundred miles south of Jacksonville, Florida. It is in the north end of Lake George, the largest lake on the St. Johns River and the second largest lake in Florida.

It is the largest island in the St. Johns River system, about seventeen hundred acres in size in a lake that is more than twenty two times as large. The St. Johns River and its tributaries drain central Florida and provide more than three hundred miles of freshwater waterways for small and larger boats from the seaport of Jacksonville in the north to near Orlando in south central Florida.

During the golden age of the steamboat, after the Civil War, the St. Johns River was the main highway to central Florida. A hotel was built on the Island in 1875 and it was gone by 1878. As railroads and highways were built into south Florida and freezes ruined the citrus growing business, farmers and tourists moved south, Drayton Island became a sparsely settled wooded bit of paradise.

The main road on Drayton Island, from the ferry landing near Georgetown on the northeast side of the island to the south-west end of the island, is about two and a half miles long. There are seven named branch roads that complete the sand road system on the Island, in some cases, long sand driveways tunnel through the pine and palmetto forest leading to waterfront clearings with mowed lawns, citrus trees, boat docks and homes. From a few places on the roads you can see the lake but most of the scenery from the road is pine and palm forests.

There are about fifty dwellings on the island spread along the lakefront and in the interior. The Island is a separate voting district in Putnam County. There were twenty one registered voters in District Four in November of 2008. Usually less than twenty one people are on the Island on a weekday night. Weekenders arrive and boost the population substantially.

From my house, on the southeast shore of the island, it is more than eleven miles to the far end of Lake George, boats disappear below the horizon as they sail south up the St. Johns River.

About thirty million people from all over the world fly over Drayton Island each year and Interstates 95 and 75 are within thirty miles of Lake George and yet, despite this, very few people know it exists. There are no mainland highways and few local roads that offer a view of Drayton Island and Lake George. Pine forests owned by Governmental agencies surround most of the lake.

There are no stores, gas stations, bars, or other commercial businesses on the Island. The county ferry, a steel barge pushed by a small boat, runs Monday and Friday, morning and evening. Islanders come and go with their own boats, or hitch a ride from a neighbor. Occasionally people will have a party and the question always comes up, "What is the history of this Island?"

-

I decided to attempt to find the answer to the question and write a little book. My high speed satellite internet dish connection gave me access to most of the world's knowledge and I began my research into the history of this Island.

Drayton Island's history is part of Florida's history and Florida's history is a most tragic soap opera.

After a few years of research into this history, I have come to the conclusion that the good old days were not so hot for the North American Indians, the imported black slaves and the indentured European immigrants. In fact, the period 1500 to 1800 was a difficult time for all of the players at every level of authority. France, Spain and Great Britain all claimed Florida at various times and maintained their claims by brute force and the blood of their rivals...

Out of the slow motion conflicts of the colonial period in North America, based in part upon the profits earned from the labor of slaves and indentured servants working the land of the Indians, the American Revolution came together and a start was made to establish a more reasonable system of Government for the 13 colonies that became the first states of the United States. The colony of Florida did not join in the revolution.

The Florida history soap opera continued after the American Revolution when, surprisingly, the United States, after defeating the

British who controlled Florida at the time, gave Florida to Spain! Spanish Florida included parts of Georgia, Alabama, Mississippi and Louisiana.

Several episodes later, the Florida history soap opera followed up with Florida becoming a territory of United States, and eventually becoming a state of the United States of America. When the Civil War commenced the State of Florida joined the Confederacy and seceded from the United States of America!

The civil war years, reconstruction, Black Codes, the KKK and the Trail of Tears followed. The costs of the racist treatment of slaves and Indians before and after the civil war are still mounting and continue to affect our nation.

Some reader is bound to observe that I do not have the education or mental marbles to write a history. I agree with the premise. However I am eighty years old and it's now or never. But it is not a history it is fiction, based upon history.

My goal is to present my impression of the information that I have found, recognizing that I may have missed the important and included the unimportant. Perhaps I made it all up. My father said, "You can learn from anyone." And, "Even a blind hog finds an acorn". He could also play the harmonica and sing, quite a trick.

My sister says I was conceived on Drayton Island in 1928, it is possible that she is correct because my family have been visiting on the island every winter for a long time. I am retired now and live on Drayton

Island, but, through the magic of the internet, I live in some new, remarkably diverse community, a virtual community. This virtual community is as unexplored and unpredictable as the Florida peninsula was when Christopher Columbus found North and South America blocking his way to the Spice Islands.

At the same time that Columbus found the new world, the twenty five million native people living in the Western Hemisphere found that they were not alone in the world. They were invaded by Europeans who brought millions of poor immigrants from Europe to settle the vast territories and 18 million black Africans to the melting pot.

The collision of cultures, the collision of men women and children that occurred in the Americas resulted in the deterioration of the ability of existing civil and religious rulers to control the masses. New forms of government and religions became established under new hierarchies.

The internet and information technology provides access and global contact to the masses, a new collision point that will also change everything. The changes will come at the speed of light, not at the speed of a sail ship.

People will identify with communities on the net rather than some narrow geographic, cultural or racial component. Many people will work at home for a company on the other side of the world.

Traditional governments and religions will be stressed to stay out in front of the changing scene. Top down has become bottom up. We can only wait, watch and listen.

Perhaps my rendering of these tales of the improbable history of Florida, Drayton Island and vicinity will provide us with some enlightenment on living together in freedom and tranquility despite the propensity of idiocy, stubbornness, greed and cruelty of our human nature, governments and religions.

This book is fiction although there may be some facts that fit. The people that I call Spanish, French, British, Catholic, Huguenot and etc. are just regular folks living in a time when taking advantage of their best options put them in the thick of it.

The same types of people are still with us doing the same mischief. In my lifetime, more than 100 million people were killed by governments or rather by people that felt some loyalty to a government. Sometimes I think we are making progress as a people and then sometimes I think we are put here on earth simply to raise the carbon dioxide level on earth for some unknown project.

Chapter 1: 1500's, Europeans Arrive in the Americas. 11

Chapter 2 Interview with Whitey Ortiz: 15

Chapter 3: 1550-1600 Spanish and the French in Florida 24

Chapter 4: Spanish Florida in the 1600's 29

Chapter 5: 1700-1763 Britain and Spain Fight for Florida 36

Chapter 6: 1763-1783 British Florida 40

Chapter 7: 1783-1819, The Second Spanish Florida 44

Chapter 8: 1819-1845 Florida, A Territory of the United States 48

Chapter 9:   1845 Florida becomes State of US 51

Chapter 10: 1863-1865   Civil War 53

Chapter 11   Zephaniah Kingsley 60

Chapter 12 Island Owners 61

Chapter 13 Quercus Virginiana a trip on the St Johns River in 1878 65

Chapter 14: A visit to Drayton Island ca1850 95

Chapter 15: Indian villages 106

Chapter 16   Working Plantation 121

Chapter 17   Places to look 04-26-2013 131

Chapter 1: 1500's, Europeans Arrive in the Americas.

The way I look at it, the men who organized and maintained the financial, political and religious power in Europe were fearful and jealous of their many competitors. They were constantly searching for opportunities to enrich their treasuries and perpetuate their dominion over the land and people. The leaders led their subjects into wars with other leaders that were a threat to their safety and treasure. The limiting factor for all of the leaders was the difficulty of maintaining control of the common people who did all of the real work and fought and died in the wars.

The leaders saw a great opportunity building and manning ships that could carry their power and influence across the seas to expand their empires and bring the riches of the new world into their treasuries. Leaders without treasure quickly lose control to competitors. The masses could be controlled by paying them to behave in a manner that supported the leaders, especially when there were no better choices.

Wooden sail ships and iron men sailed across the seas guided by the stars and a belief they were doing God's work by serving their king. They brought slaves, horses, chickens and pigs to the new world; they wore armor and used guns. They enslaved or killed many of the Indians and stole their gold. They did not just do this in the Americas; they did it around Africa to India and Asia.

They brought millions of Africans to slavery in the new world. They enticed millions of common people to emigrate from poor countries in Europe to seek their fortunes in the new land. The great powers of Europe fought each other for dominance as they slowly colonized the Americas and other parts of the globe to enrich their kings and queens. Most of the world population was serfs with little chance of the good life.

Spain, Britain, Netherlands, Portugal, France and other nations spread their influence around the globe in search of new lands and people to conquer and claim as their own. Independent adventurers sailed the seas with or without the open or secret support of the rulers to capture enemy ships and to attack enemy colonies.

In that time, there were no easy methods of communication between the rulers and their forces. The commanders of the forces in the field or at sea were on their own with no means of asking for help or guidance in time of trouble. These commanders were ruthless and did what they had to do to survive. At times, they operated for years without direction making their own rules.

During the early years of the fifteen hundreds, men loyal to Spain established influence in Florida, Mexico, Peru, Puerto Rico, Hispaniola, Cuba, Central America and Argentina. They established ports on the Atlantic and Pacific Oceans in Mexico and Central America and established regular trade routes to the Far East and the west coast of South America. As they expanded their influence and lengthened their trade routes they became more vulnerable to attack.

The native people of North and South America were not immune to European diseases and the populations were devastated by these diseases and the harsh treatment by the Spaniards. Many Indians were made slaves to work the mines and fields under the direction of the Spanish. Indian deaths from disease and maltreatment created a shortage of labor.

The Spanish began importing African slaves to work the mines and plantations. In 1574 there were 12 slaves to every Spaniard on Hispaniola. Gold was mined on the island. Gold was, as it is now, easy to transport and is highly valued.

An important influence on the Spanish was the Catholic Religion. It was difficult to determine if there was a difference between the Spanish Government and the Church. An important goal was to spread the Catholic religion. Priests were sent to establish missions as part of the Spanish invasions of the new territories.

The soldiers had orders to kill or enslave the heretics that would not accept Catholicism. The first goal, however, was to acquire gold and other riches to support the rulers.

In 1500, the Florida peninsula was an unexplored mystery to the Europeans. Control of Florida was important to Spain's security as their ships traveled the Straits of Florida. Ships loaded with gold and silver from South America and the Caribbean islands, bound for Spain, were vulnerable to pirates based in any of the many harbors on the coast of Florida.

Several Spanish expeditions to Florida were organized to explore and claim Florida for Spain. One night I interviewed Whitey Ortiz who was part of one of the expeditions.

(Yes, you read it correctly! How else can you explain Whitey's story being here in this book. I woke up one morning and typed out the following interview.)

Chapter 2 Interview with Whitey Ortiz:

My name is Whitey Ortiz and I was born in Barcelona Spain in the year 1500. I never went to school. At the age of 14, I was impressed as a crew member on a ship bound for Cuba. On the voyage, I met several soldiers and their commander. We got on well together and I decided to join them. On arrival at Cuba, I was a part of the troop. While at Cuba we served at the wishes of the Governor of the island now known as Cuba.

Ponce Deleon, who was recovering from wounds inflicted by Indians during an ill fated exploration searching for gold in Florida, visited Cuba seeking an appointment to a post that did not include fighting Indians. While recovering from his wounds, he was assigned to the post of Governor of Puerto Rico.

In 1518, our troop was assigned to Luke Velasquez and we sailed from Cuba on an expedition to St. Helena in what is now the State of South Carolina. We anchored in the bay and sent boats ashore to meet the Indians and to supply the ship with provisions.

Captain Velasquez got on well with the Indians and he invited a great number of them to come aboard the ship for a party. When the Indians were all on board, we seized them and bound them in chains. Some of the astonished Indians jumped overboard and swam for the shore. As they swam for the shore we opened fire on them and killed many and wounded many more.

We stowed the Indians below decks and sailed back to Cuba. In Cuba, Captain Luke Velasquez sold the Indians as slaves and made a pretty penny. The Indians cried and moaned the whole voyage and some of them died of a broken heart, others starved themselves to death.

Captain Luke Velasquez made another trip to the same place, for the same purpose, two years later in 1520 with a different crew. I was now working in Cuba, in the jail as a guard. He took two ships and more than two hundred soldiers to St. Helena.

This time the Indians decoyed the troops away from the beach and the Indians attacked and killed most of the soldiers. The remainder fled to the boats and put to sea.

On the return trip, the Spanish ships encountered a terrible storm and were shipwrecked and all perished except Luke Velasquez himself. He was picked up by a passing ship and returned to Spain to pass the rest of his life in misery and regret for his failure.

Around 1524, everyone believed there was plenty of gold in Florida, and the Spanish King, who had never been near the place, granted Frances de Guerray all of Florida but Guerray died before he could do anything about it.

Guerray was succeeded by Allyon who raised forces and invaded the peninsula. Instead of gold mines, he found swamps filled with armed savages ready to attack them at every natural defile. He lost half of his men and fled from the insect ridden Florida peninsula filled with aggressive Indians.

In 1528, I was a horse soldier and was tired of duty in Cuba. I volunteered along with about 500 others to join Pamphillo de Narves to seek our fortunes in the search for gold in Florida and the lands to the North. We landed in what is now Charlotte Bay and Pamphillo claimed all of the land for the King of Spain.

We did not see any Indians the first few days but we saw many deserted villages of wigwams. We traveled north through woods and swamps to another bay where we found some Indians. These Indians had some corn which they gave to us. They also had wooden cases containing dead Indians covered with skins ornamented with sprigs of gold. We were informed that the gold came from Appalache. Pamphillo, against advice, ordered us to ride north to find the gold. He provisioned us with two pounds of biscuits and half a pound of pork per soldier...

For fifteen days we traveled through a desolate country void of inhabitants and food. We crossed a large river partly by swimming and partly by rafts and we found some Indians but no gold. The Indians had a village and we stayed 25 days in the area taking food from the Indians to survive.

We were forced to deal harshly with the Indians because they resented our presence. We chained up the Chief and some of his men. The Indians raided us by night and killed or stole our horses. We finally attacked their town of Auta and captured a great quantity of corn, peas, gourds and fruits that were consumed by our starving men

An exploring party was dispatched to examine the coastline and they returned with the news that the sea was a few days distant surrounded by dismal swamps and marshes. All of our men were weak and most of the horses were gone. We marched down to the sea fighting off the savages every night. We were losing men each day.

At the shore, we killed all of the remaining horses, made boats of their hides and twisted ropes of the hair of their manes and tails. We cut up our shirts for sails and by the 22nd of September set sail in five boats on a course towards Mexico.

We made little progress and wandered for seven days before reaching open sea. We caught plenty of fish but could find no fresh water. We were afraid to enter the back country searching for water.

We met some coastal Indians, finally, that gave us food and water and they seemed friendly. During the night, the Indians mounted a fierce attack on us and rescued the imprisoned chief. Panphillo received a grave wound in the fight and we retreated to the boats.

During a storm, the boats became separated and my boat was cast up on an Island. I was rescued and returned to Cuba.

In Cuba, they thought I was very lucky to have survived the ordeal and was called upon to tell the story many times of our adventures.

Panphillo de Narvaez's wife heard me tell the story and she prevailed upon me to undertake an expedition to look for her husband who might still be living on the Florida Coast. She offered me a great deal of money to undertake the search and I thought that, if I succeeded, I would become an important person.

Fitted out with a small pinnace I sailed back to the hostile coast. It was not long before I was taken prisoner by the Indians and tied to a stake in the village. The Indian women of the village were curious about the white prisoner; they poked me with sticks and threw mud at me. The Indians were going to kill me for sure.

After a few days I found that the daughter of the chief had taken a fancy to me and wanted me as a slave. To make a long story short, I lived with her for several years and we had two children. I was assigned duties by the chief and one of them was defending the burial ground. A wolf disinterred a body and although I had killed the wolf, I was sentenced to death.

My wife released me and directed me to travel south until I reach Tampa Bay. At Tampa Bay I would find Macaco, the chief. He was powerful, a friend of hers, and he would protect me from her father. I lived in the villages of Macaco for twelve years or so and learned to be an

Indian and to speak the languages. I taught the Indians what I knew about horses, pigs, tools, utensils and guns.

I left the Indians in 1539 when Ferdinand Desoto's army came close to my village. A few Indian friends and I made ourselves known to the leaders and I became a trusted interpreter, scout and officer in Desoto's army.

Desoto had distinguished himself in the conquest of Peru. The proprietors of the mines were glad to send him on his way with a million and a half dollars in gold because they regarded him with suspicion.

The King of Spain agreed that Desoto should avenge the destruction of his countrymen by the Florida Indians and redeem the national honor.

Desoto purchased seven ships and three cutters which he armed and equipped for the expedition. He enlisted one thousand men, three hundred of them were cavaliers well mounted on excellent horses. We brought two hundred twenty horses and three hundred hogs. He also had many slaves to carry the stuff.

He sailed for Cuba and while there he married the sister of the famous Bovadilla. He filled out his expedition with 200 slaves and sailed for Tampa Bay in Florida.

I had cautioned Desoto that the best plan was to not molest the Indians and to make friends with them. The Indians had many cattle and much corn and could be a great help to the expedition.

Despite several incidents of violence and the return of Captain Porcello to Cuba, we managed to gain the friendship of two chiefs who controlled the land south of Orlando.

We marched north into the province of Ocala. For thirty miles we marched through a country of tall pines, the Indian population was dense, for some leagues the houses were thickly scattered along the road. Ocala contained six hundred houses. The chief was friendly and supplied us with provisions. The country was spotted with ponds and small streams.

We reached the town of Chichile in the province of Vitachucco, south of the Alachua Prairie. It was fortified with palisades and contained five hundred houses. The chiefs' house was 120 feet long and had many rooms and was built on an artificial hill. It was here that Desoto departed from the pacific course which he had hitherto pursued toward the natives.

The last words that I remember hearing from Whitey were,

"I was killed by an Indian."

Author's Note:

I asked Whitey, if, while marching north of Ocala, he went to the St. Johns River and Lake George. He said that the Indians told him of the great lake and the Indian village on the Island known as Edelano, however he did not see it himself.

Desoto's expedition continued for four years, until July of 1543 when the haggard remnant of his troops arrived to relative safety in Mexico. Desoto died in Texas in May of 1542 after traveling through 12 or 14 states and exploring parts of the Mississippi River.

His expedition stunned the Indians. War, pain and death were nothing new to the Indians, but the Spanish attitude that they were doing the work of God killing the heathens was brutal and barbaric. Desoto found no gold and did not defeat the Indians. The Spanish treatment of the Indians was never forgotten.

During the next decades many men like Whitey spread the cultural knowledge across the barriers between the Indians and the Spanish. Deadly diseases crossed between the cultures along with the knowledge. The Indians rapidly gained guns, horses and slaves from the Spanish invaders. Within a century the Indians had horses and guns and knew how to use them.

During the first 50 years of the 1500's the Europeans did not have a substantial permanent presence in Florida. Most of the Indians had never seen a European. Some parts of Florida were visited by groups of unorganized hunters and fishermen from the Caribbean Islands and by pirates and other fugitives that lived off the land and salvaging wrecks. Florida, then as now, is a haven for people that like the sun, the easy life and freedom.

Chapter 3: 1550-1600 Spanish and the French in Florida

The Spanish ships loaded with treasures collected from the Spanish outposts in Central and South America passed through the Florida Straits. They coasted up along the Florida peninsula to catch the westerlies, the winds that would bring them home. It became more and more important for the Spanish to secure the safety of these ships.

The British and the French, although stressed to the breaking point maintaining their interests around the world, endeavored to interrupt the Spanish success in finding treasures and holding territories in the new world.

Both The British and the French were faced with people at home that were unsatisfied with the state religions and the Kings saw colonies as the solution. If the religious dissenters could be sent overseas, they would be out of sight and mind.

Spain and France, both, decided to send colonists to Florida at about the same time. I have interviewed Pierre de Angelbert who will shed some light on the situation in 1563.

Interview with Pierre DeAngelbert

My name is Pierre:

I am a Frenchman, not a sailor, but a musician, assigned to the Admirals retinue as part of the orchestra. Four of us played for the officers at dinner and on special occasions. We were assigned to fire fighting below decks in battle conditions. We also played cards and entertained the officers during the long voyages.

In the year 1563 I sailed with Admiral Jean Ribault and Vice Admiral Laudeniere to Charlesfort in the new world (Near present day Parris island ,SC) to establish a settlement. The voyage out and back took 2 months.

I learned that, on a previous voyage, Admiral Ribault had explored the great southern river that is now known as St. Johns and claimed the land for France.

The year following my trip with Admiral Ribault, Vice Admiral Laudeniere requested that I accompany him on a voyage to the St. Johns River to establish a settlement. We sailed with three ships and more than 300 settlers, soldiers and sailors along with all of the supplies required to establish a settlement.

The Indians welcomed us when we arrived in the St. Johns River and they brought us to the place that Admiral Ribault had established a monument commemorating that this land belonged to the King of France. They gave us food and helped us build shelters. Compared to the Spaniards, the French were accepted as friends by the Indians.

-

Vice Admiral Laudeniere had trouble from the start with the Huguenot settlers. They did not obey orders and refused to start the work on the gardens required to produce food. Some of the settlers left with a small boat and they became pirates in the Gulf.

Laudeniere bought a ship from John Hawkins, a British privateer, and sent some of the settlers back to France in an effort to get rid of the non-cooperative members.

In 1565, Admiral Ribault himself arrived from France with a fleet of ships and 600 more Huguenot settlers. He stood offshore to wait for the higher spring tides that were due in seven days. He and Laudeniere had a disagreement over who would command the colony. Laudeniere lost the argument and agreed to return to France and leave the colony to Admiral Jean Ribault.

Before the Vice Admiral Laudeniere could leave, Menendez Aviles, the Spanish Commander arrived offshore with a fleet of ships and 800 settlers, soldiers and sailors. The French and the Spanish fleets began to prepare to fight to the finish. The pre-hurricane sea conditions made it impossible to carry on the battle and Menendez sailed south into St. Augustine harbor to seek shelter from the storm.

Ribault also sailed south with most of the soldiers and left Laudeniere at Fort Caroline with 20 soldiers and 100 men and women. The hurricane drove the French ships south and the ships were wrecked on the beach south of St. Augustine. Many drowned but most gathered on the beach. Admiral Ribault gathered his men and the French Huguenots together and started walking north along the narrow spit of land. He hoped he could convince Menendez to allow his men to return to France.

Admiral Menendez Aviles during height of the hurricane sent his men from St. Augustine, north overland 40 miles and made a surprise attack on Ft. Caroline. His men killed all of the Huguenot men but spared 40 women and children as slaves. In the confusion, Laudeniere managed to escape with 40-50 others. He made his way to the rivers mouth where Renaults' son was anchored in a sheltered cove. Laudeniere made his way back to France with Renault's son with the bad news.

A Spanish beach patrol from St. Augustine discovered the French castaways and captured them. Menendez ordered his men to kill all of the heretics including Admiral Ribault. Three hundred and fifty men were executed, put to the knife. A few self professing Christians and the musicians including me were spared.

Author's Note: The military power of France on the Florida Coast was never again a force to be reckoned with. France gave up the idea of colonizing Florida. What happened to Pierre? I do not know, but there is a famous French musician of the same name.

Spain in 1550 staged a new world version of the Spanish Inquisition in Mexico City. Only a few people were tortured and killed but the public ceremonies were noticed throughout New Spain.

For the next hundred years Spain was the dominant European power in and around Florida. Actually, the Indians controlled the interior and much of the coastline and traded with the Spanish.

There is a difference in effort, capital, knowledge and chutzpah required to establish permanent colonies in the new land compared to the establishment of limited military posts primarily supported by supply lines from across the seas.

The lessons learned and techniques developed while establishing a colony can be transferred from colony to colony but each colony presents unique problems and opportunities that require careful problem solving.

Chapter 4: Spanish Florida in the 1600's

The Florida that Spain claimed extended from the Mississippi River on the west including Georgia on the east coast. It included the southern portion of what are now Louisiana, Mississippi, & Alabama and all of Florida and Georgia. Throughout this vast territory, a Spanish presence was maintained through Missions that were established to convert Indians to Catholicism, and to monitor trade with the Indians. The Spanish military provided soldiers to man the widely dispersed forts and the navy protected the sea lanes.

The missions brought Europeans to the territory and the Europeans brought diseases that devastated the Indians. As an example, when Cortez invaded Mexico his victory over the Aztecs was in part made possible by a smallpox epidemic among the Indians. Everywhere the Europeans went they unknowingly brought diseases that decimated the Indians.

In eastern Florida the main Spanish Settlement was the city of St Augustine. Many of the Spanish Land Grants to loyal subjects were between the Atlantic coast and the St. Johns River north and south of the City of St. Augustine. This area was suitable for settlement and the settlers could flee to the city in case of attack by other European powers, independent pirates or by Indians.

Drayton Island or Edelano Island as it was called by the Indians at that time, on the St. Johns, is less than 50 miles from St. Augustine and has no record of development, except by Indians, until the mid 1700's. Jose Hernandez was granted land at the North end of Lake George and may have used the island as range land for pigs, cattle and goats. According to the evidence found in shell mounds on the island, Indians lived on the island for thousands of years before the Europeans appeared in Florida.

Picolata, on the St. Johns, about 17 miles from St. Augustine, and 40 miles downriver from Drayton Island, served as the closest access point from St. Augustine to the river. The St. Johns River provided a navigable waterway to the interior of Florida from present day Orlando in the south to Jacksonville in the north, a river distance of more than 250 miles.

Overland travel was difficult because there were few roads, thick forests, swamps and creeks impeded travel. Traveling on the river was also difficult. Boats propelled by sails relied on wind. When there was no wind or the wind blew in the wrong direction the boats had to be polled or rowed. The river depth varied from many feet to a few inches on the sand bars. A trip from St. Augustine to Drayton Island might take 3 or 4 days including a couple of nights camping on the river bank.

There were many attacks by pirates and Indians on St. Augustine during this period. The Spanish built a fort called Castillo de San Marco using Indian and Slave labor. The fort was in the town and overlooked the harbor.

The Spanish built another settlement at Pensacola in west Florida at the end of the century. Communication between Pensacola and St. Augustine required a long overland journey fraught with danger to the courier or a long voyage, also fraught with danger, around the Florida peninsula by sail ship. The vast territory and long coastline of Florida was largely unguarded and uninhabited. Pirates, escaped slaves, Indians and freemen all found Florida an inviting place to escape the laws and harsh treatment of Spain, England and France. They came from the Caribbean Islands, Mexico, Virginia, Carolina Cuba, Hispaniola and the Bahamas. They made salt, fished, caught turtles, salvaged wrecks and sold bird feathers and animal skins.

During this Spanish period in Florida, the British established colonies north of Florida. In 1607 the British settled Massachusetts and Jamestown, Virginia with indentured colonists with poor results, some colonists died by starvation in 1609, in 1622 an Indian massacre of colonists occurred and by 1624 43% of the colonists had died.

The first African slaves were brought in 1619. In 1676, 80% of the non-slave people were indentured servants unhappy with the terms of their indenture. They rebelled against the British. In 1691. This was the period of the Salem Witch trials.

The British established Carolina in 1670 with settlers from Barbados and they invited Protestants, Baptists, Quakers, Huguenots, Jews, and Presbyterians to settle to prevent the Catholics from taking over. The Carolina upcountry was settled by Scots-Irish immigrants from

Pennsylvania and Virginia. Imported African Slaves became the majority of the population in some southern colonies.

From 1670-1717 British traders conducted trade in American Indian slaves. The slaves were bought from Indian tribes in the western wilderness. They exported as many as 50,000 slaves during the period. The Yamasee Indian War (1715-1717) put an end to the Indian Slave business and seriously threatened the existence of the colony.

After the Carolina Yamasee war, the British planters used African slaves exclusively because of their expertise in raising and processing rice and indigo and the general acceptance of the ownership of black slaves by the British Government.

Spanish claims to the territory of Mexico included a territory so large that it would include most of modern day California on the North and Peru on the South. Estimates of Mexican Indian population before the Spanish conquest ranged from 6 to 25 million. Spain was active in the slave trade in all of their colonies.

The French claimed the land drained by the Mississippi between the British Colonies and the Spanish Mexico.

The Spanish built the Fort in St. Augustine using slaves and hired laborers, some of which were Indians.

I Interviewed Turtle-Son:

-

My name is turtle-son, I was born on Edelano Island in your year 1650, I was of the Utina or Timuqua tribe and lived on the west side of the river you now call St. Johns near the seven mile spring. The Spanish made a gift of Edelano to a Spanish nobleman and forced us to move off the island onto the forest near the spring.

In the fall of the year 1672 I left my family and went to St. Augustine to work for the Spaniards in the quarry on Anastasia Island.

The Spanish brought many slaves from Mexico and Africans from Cuba to work on the Fort. We, members of our tribe, worked in the quarry cutting the stones all through the winter. The quarry was too hot in mid- summer.

The stone was called coquina and was a soft stone when quarried. We would cut the blocks and stack them for a year or so in the sun to harden them. We were paid piece work and worked with little supervision.

We were not allowed to go to the fort or to talk with the slaves that were building the fort. The overseers of the slaves treated them very badly and many of them died from their punishments. The lived in the fort in the rooms built into the walls of the fort. They worked every day and spent the nights locked in the rooms.

Our tribe, worked every winter for twenty years in the quarry. We lived in the quarry in the winter and moved back to the spring in the summer. Other Indians tribes sent men to work with us in the quarry. We were all free and not considered slaves.

When we worked, we were paid in credits that could be redeemed at the trading posts that were established by the Spanish traders. Our chief made a special side deal with the Spanish and he doubtless was paid some small amount for each stone. The traders sold the Indians rum and the Indians would get drunk for two or three days.

Many of our tribe fell ill with the fever and most that contracted the disease died. As we lost members of our tribe, we consolidated our villages, and abandoned many, to the northern Indians and escaped slaves that were not originally from Florida but from lands to the north and west. These were known as Seminoles and were warlike raiding the colonists along the river. Some of these Indians were hired out by the Spanish to attack Appalachie Indians and to steal their cows and pigs. The Spanish stayed near the fort and left the woods to the Indians. If groups of Indians came into the town area the Spanish would. Send the soldiers to chase us away.

Many of our tribe agreed to be Christians and were baptized by the Jesuit fathers. The missionary fathers would order the Christian Indians to work in the Mission gardens and to bring deer and turtles to the mission.

Authors Comment:

This chapter covers the years 1600 through 1700. The Spanish had nominal control of Florida during this period. Sporadic attacks by Pirates and others were repulsed or discouraged. Rather than colonizing or developing this hot worthless area, the goal seemed to be preventing others from controlling this strategic territory. Traders, small farmers, fishermen, pirates and others that get along with the Indians established themselves in the vast territory without interference from the Spanish.

Chapter 5: 1700-1763 Britain and Spain Fight for Florida

The British colonies north of Florida continue to grow in population as immigrants arrive from Europe and the children of settlers start their own families and move westward in search for new land to cultivate. This expansion of the land under cotton cultivation in the south increased the demand for African slaves to work the fields. The population of African slaves continued to increase in the areas where cotton could be planted.

British slave traders captured and enslaved many American Indians for export. The slave traders also destabilized the Indian population by offering to buy slaves from the Indian tribes friendly to the British. The pressures by settlers for new land resulted in treaties between the Indians and the settlers granting land to the settlers in return for promises. These treaties were made, from time to time, for 100 years and in the end the Indians were driven out of eastern North America.

The Spanish laws regarding slaves and Indians were less harsh than the British laws in Virginia and Carolina, many escaped slaves and Indians found their way into Florida. These people moved into the areas originally occupied by the Florida Indians. The Florida Indian tribes had been decimated by disease, war and assimilation into other groups. The Seminoles, as these wanderers were called, were not the naive natives that Columbus found but were the result of 250 years of contact &

-

conflict with the Europeans. They could be equal or better than the Europeans on an individual basis but they lacked the capital and power of empire.

The British colonists felt that the Spanish enticed their slaves to run away. In 1702 British troops from South Carolina invaded Florida and marched to St. Augustine. They sack and burn the city but are unable to overcome the fort.

Two years later other troops returned to Florida and destroyed all of the Franciscan Missions in Florida. The British killed or enslaved the Florida Indians that were friendly with the Spanish. For a time, the British were allied with the Yamasee Indians and encouraged them to capture and enslave Florida Indians. The Florida Indians were further decimated by these depredations. The Yamasee Indians, finally fed up with the British, revolted against the British in the early 1700's.

The British increased the importation of African Slaves. British companies and traders dominated the Atlantic Slave trade for quite a long time but many other companies were involved in trading about 18 million African people across the Atlantic to the new world. The slave trade in Africa still exists today, in a small way, however the slave trade destabilized every part of Africa by enriching tribal leaders who supplied the slaves in return for guns and money that could be used to maintain their absolute power over the tribes.

Georgia is settled in 1732 by colonists from the debtor's prisons in Britain. In the beginning the colony had laws against slavery but it soon became evident that slaves were a requirement to run profitable plantations. By 1742 Spain and England are locked in a Global struggle for supremacy. The British capture St. Augustine and the St. Marys River becomes the border between Spanish Florida and British Georgia. Britain occupies Quebec, Prince Edward Island and Cuba.

1763 Britain traded away Cuba to Spain in return for Florida after the end of the Seven Years War.

The treaty of Paris in 1763 simplified my understanding of why Spain gave Florida to Britain. It seems that in the mid 1750's the countries of Spain, Austria, Russia, Sweden and others joined up on the green team and the blue team was Great Britain, Prussia, Portugal, and others. The teams fought a war called the Seven Years War. Towards the end of the seven years they tired of the expense and decided to hold a Texas hold'em game in Paris.

When the game was over they all agreed to a new alignment of the ownership of the world. The funny thing was that many of the teams were ruled by the same families. The same gang controlled the Churches, the money and the courthouse.

When the residents of Florida heard that the British owned Florida, nearly all of the Spanish residents fled to other Spanish colonies because of the British laws pertaining to race, religion and slavery.

-

No one knew that, within twenty years, an event would occur that would forever change the balance of power in the new world and the old world. The huddled masses, yearning to be free, would form a representative government with no hereditary offices and throw out the British.

Chapter 6: 1763-1783 British Florida

This chapter is about a twenty year period in the history of Florida during which time Spain is thrown out, Britain is finally successful in controlling all of the colonies from the Mississippi River in the west to the rocky coast of Maine in the east and all of the coastline from the Mississippi River, around Florida up to Maine and most of the Canadian coast too. It looked like the British would own all of North America.

Now getting back to the Story, Britain won Florida in the poker game known as the Treaty of Paris of 1763. The Spanish colonists left Florida to the Indians, escaped slaves, pirates and people that thought they could get along with British rule... The British divided Florida into West Florida with Pensacola as the capital and East Florida with St. Augustine as the capital.

The British began an intense effort to recruit people to settle in the Florida colony that included parts of Alabama, Mississippi and Louisiana. The British offered free land for farmers and financial backing for export oriented businesses. They gave land to well connected people that never set foot in Florida.

Cotton, rice and indigo were crops that could be exported with high profits to the shipping and financial interests in Britain and could also provide tariff and tax income to the colonies. The British colonial laws were brought to the Florida colonies. Slavery was OK.

William Drayton Sr. a Carolina judge educated in London was appointed Chief Justice of East Florida by Patrick Tonyn the Governor of British East Florida. During Drayton's fifteen year stay in Florida he acquired many properties. Drayton Island was one of the properties. He did not do anything with the Island.

Many British started new Plantations in East Florida between the St. Johns River and St. Augustine. Indentured servants from Scotland, England and Eastern Europe by the thousands were recruited. Many of these plantations were successful but many failed because of bad management and poor locations. Field work in the summer in Florida is very difficult. The Europeans, in general, were not able to do the work as well as black African slaves. Slaves and Indentured servants who wish for the failure of the project do not make good workers and they can easily sabotage a crop or project despite an alert overseer.

A man named Spaulding established two trading posts on the west side of the St. Johns River to establish trade with the Indians. Drayton Island was located between the upper and lower stores. Mrs. Spaulding made a solitary trip from the Carolinas in a boat with four slaves. The slaves rowed and sailed the boat for many days.

Continue: William Bartram recorded visiting Drayton Island about this time and finding an abandoned Indian village and no people. He also recorded a stop at Spaulding's Upper Store and visiting friendly Indians villages far west of the river. He also reported that the Indians spent seven days drinking whiskey obtained by trading furs. The Indians drank seven days, the traders drank every day.

By 1768 the British set up a Southern Military headquarters at St Augustine in anticipation of a possible revolution in the British colonies. When the revolution started in 1776, many colonists from the thirteen colonies seeking independence that were loyal to Britain fled to Florida with all of their slaves and possessions. They were given free land by the Governor of East Florida. Most of these English Plantations in East Florida were east of the St. Johns and within 50 miles of St. Augustine.

The thirteen colonies of NH, MA, CO, RI, NY, PA, NJ, DE, MD, VA, NC, SC, and GA asserted their independence from Britain and the revolution began. The Colonies of East and West Florida did not assert their independence and remained loyal to Britain. Britain was actively at war with the Spanish and French at the same time as the revolution.

As a culmination of the revolution, the second Treaty of Paris in 1783 resulted in the thirteen colonies gaining their independence. I will not go into all of the other deals made at the treaty but I will say that Spain walked out with Florida in its pocket. The United States gave Florida to Spain!

The British colonists in Florida are about to boosted out just as they boosted out the Spanish twenty years before. By this time just about everyone is broke and desperate. The colonists are about to lose everything, the Indians that made friends with the British are going to be roasted by the Spanish, the slaves are going to be loaded in a boat and taken to some new place that will probably be worse if possible. The majority of the people will be unemployed, their money will be worthless.

Drayton island still is just sitting in the lake, birds are singing, fish are jumping, not a soul in sight.

In 1783, at the end of this twenty year period, George Washington is now President of the original British thirteen colonies that are now the United States of America. Britain is thrown out of all of the lands south of Canada and Florida is back in the hands of the Spanish.

As Imus says, "You can't make it up."

Chapter 7: 1783-1819, The Second Spanish Florida

Let's recap the Florida Timeline:

1500-1763, 263 years, the first Spanish Period
(French Colony on St. Johns River 1562-1565)

1763-1783, 20 years, the British Period

1783-1819, 36 years, the Second Spanish Period

1819-1845, 26 years, Florida Territory of the U.S.

In 1783, after the Revolution that resulted in the United States of America, at the beginning of this second period of Spanish rule of Florida, just about everyone was surprised that Florida reverted to Spanish rule.

All of the British government people, the plantation owners and the settlers that did not want to be Catholic or live under Spanish law were packing their bags. The ownership of land under the British law would not necessarily be recognized by the Spanish.

They could not travel by steamboat or trains because these had not been invented or were not available. Sailing ship freight rates were high and there was no place to go on a horse so they left a lot of their stuff behind. Most were financially ruined.

All of the deals made by the Indians with the British were unenforceable. The Spanish were the boss again. They owned the courthouse. The only problem was that the Spanish really did not have their heart in Florida and did not spend much effort establishing a new society. They passed out land grants to any and all comers that would settle in Florida. Hundreds of foreigners and U. S. citizens took advantage of the land grants. The Spanish tax collectors assessed taxes on slaves, merchandise, wagons, real estate and other measurable assets owned by the residents of Florida.

The vast interior of Florida also became a haven for escaped slaves and displaced Indians. The raids by these people based in Florida against the plantations in the United States were a serious problem to the United States.

American settlers moved south, gained a foothold in Florida and ignored the Spanish laws and taxes. The American settlers in Spanish Florida plotted the takeover of Florida. Dan McGirth a leader of the settlers formed an alliance with Indians and with two hundred riders he harassed Spanish colonial forces along the St. Johns River. His cavalry moved quickly, they struck the Spaniard troops and disappeared into the pine woods. His horse was named Grey Goose and it could swim like a duck.

John McIntosh and about two hundred landowners between the St. Johns and the St. Marys Rivers seceded from Spain and formed a short lived provisional Independent Government of East Florida. Some say they were encouraged by President Madison.

In 1812 Britain and the United States and other countries outlawed the African Slave Trade. With the new supply of slaves cut off, the existing slaves became more valuable and slaves were encouraged to have large families to increase the supply of slaves.

The law that prohibited African slave trade did not stop the trading of African slaves that were already in the pipeline. The United States law declared all children of slaves must be slaves forever.

Some say that President Madison encouraged raiders from Georgia and South Carolina to stage a Patriots Rebellion. They marched into Florida and besieged St. Augustine. The Spanish hired some Seminole Indians to drive out the Patriots.

Both sides were in a bad mood, when they withdrew up the St. Johns River they burned all of the plantations found along the river. It is possible that they burned the beginnings of a plantation that Zephaniah Kingsley was building on Drayton Island. They burned ZK's other plantation at Doctors Lake and they captured ZK for ransom. In 1817 General Andrew Jackson with United States Troops invaded Florida chasing runaway slaves and Seminole Indians, he cut a wide swath. From that point on, United States effectively controlled East Florida. This is the same Andrew Jackson that became President of the United States and, among other things, moved the Indians to the west in the movement that became known as the Trail of Tears. The Indians were given more promises about the wonderful life they would have in the desert like Indian Territory.

How about this? President Jackson's vice president was John C. Calhoun, Calhoun's son; Jr. purchased Drayton Island from George Kingsley's estate. Calhoun had financial problems and Drayton Island was sold at auction. It was sold to a friend of President Jackson, Duff Green.

In 1791 the slaves in Haiti revolted against the French and established the first independent Government of African Americans in the new world. The slaves overcame Polish Troops hired to fight for the French. A new two caste black Government arose. Some world organization approved and imposed reparations to France for their loss of Haiti and the Haitians finally paid off the debt in 1946, Haiti was the most profitable colony in the world before the revolution. Since the revolution Haiti has been poor. It is interesting that the slave value of the residents of Haiti was added in to the French reparations.

They say that Napoleon was influenced by the Haiti revolution to sell Louisiana to the United States.

Chapter 8: 1819-1845 Florida, A Territory of the United States

In 1819 there was a sitting down and they called it the Adams-Onis Treaty. I do not know what game they played but this time the United States walked out with Florida in its pocket and Spain got an IOU saying the United States would not claim Texas. This upstart United States was learning how to play the game. (Despite the solemn promise, we all know Texas became a State!)

U. S. General Andrew Jackson had already invaded and taken possession of Florida under the guise of searching for escaped slaves and renegade Indians. Two subjects that made the average guys blood boil.

About this time a new invention was being introduced that was made to order for the St. Johns River. The steamboats time had come and nobody was going to stop it. Steamboats were so popular on the St. Johns that a Jacksonville observer in 1833 wrote that there was never a time when a steamboat was not visible. The three hundred mile river system was lined with farms and plantations and towns. The St. Johns was the main street of interior central Florida.

In 1790, the United States census without Florida totaled 16.5 million people. There were 2,201,420 slaves; there were 350,000 free blacks and 13,671,420 others. To give you a sense of the population of Florida, the first U.S. Census in 1830 counted 18,395 white persons and

16,335 Non White persons. In 1830 the 11 confederate states produced more cotton than all of the other countries in the world combined. .

Those pesky Indians were still a thorn in the side of the Florida territory settlers so they had a powwow with some of the Indians and came up with the Treaty of Moultrie Creek in 1823. The Seminoles, in return for some bling stuff and a reservation in the center of Florida beginning at Lake George south along the St. Johns River, guaranteed for 20 years, gave up all claims to Florida.

In 1828 Andrew Jackson was elected President and in 1830 the Congress passed the Indian Removal Act. The Indians cried foul. So they made a new Treaty called the Treaty at Payne's Landing that was "wonderful and fair" and in the end the Indians said that they were not sure they had signed the Treaty and besides it was not fair. They then tried the Fort Gibson Treaty but finally negotiations broke down and the second Seminole War began in 1835.

In 1835 U.S. troops from Tampa went up the Kings highway to Ocala (Fort King) and they were attacked by the Seminoles. One Hundred and seven soldiers were killed and three survived. Three Indians were killed and five were wounded. The war dragged on to 1842 with no settlement or capitulation.

In 1842 the Congress passed the Armed Settlement Act that gave free land to settlers that would live on and improve the land. Sounds like if they killed a few Indians that would be a plus.

Chapter 9: 1845 Florida becomes State of US

Florida Territory became a State of The United States of America in 1845, after being a Territory for about 23 years. The borders of the original colonies and the territory surrounding the colonies were subjects of conflicting claims for many years. No one disputed that Florida extends from the beaches of the Gulf of Mexico to the beaches of the Atlantic Ocean, but the northern border with Georgia was a source of conflict. Both Georgia and Florida originally claimed the west to the Mississippi River. The legislatures of the various States and the Federal Government were filled with supporters of different interests. The addition of the Louisiana Purchase and the Spanish lands to the west of the Louisiana Purchase provided many hours of conflict as the United States expanded westward. The belief of "Manifest Destiny", that the United States was destined to expand throughout the continent, drove the expansion of the number of states.

Conflict was accepted as a normal and the imperialist expansion proved to be inevitable, sweeping away opposition with compromise and conflict. The slavery question was papered over by the admittance of free and slave states, Florida, and Texas were admitted as slave states and were more or less balanced in a few years by Iowa, Michigan and Minnesota.

The Civil War settled the slavery question but it did not settle the problems that arose when 44% of the population became free. Free to do what?

Florida was the least populous Southern State, in 1900 its population was only 529,000; 44% were African American and 56% were non African American.

Chapter 10: 1863-1865   Civil War

February 1864

The complete naval blockade of the long coastline of the Confederate States was one part of the strategy of the Union naval forces during the war of secession. The second part of the strategy was to gain control of the Mississippi River, dividing the Confederacy in two.

The Confederate economy was primarily agricultural and relied upon imports of manufactured goods from Europe to carry on the war of secession. The export of cotton to Europe was the main source of foreign exchange for the confederacy. The Union blockade was designed to prevent all Confederate imports and exports. However, the thousands of miles of coastline, especially the coastline of Florida, provided blockade runners ample opportunity to carry out trade using small boats that sailed to the Caribbean Islands, Cuba and Bermuda, all controlled by Britain.

The St. Johns River, in Florida, and its tributaries such as the Oklawaha River, provided a navigable river system extending some 250 miles to the south of the Jacksonville inlet and served as an inland transportation artery for goods smuggled into or out of the Confederacy. Goods could be transported overland between the river and the Atlantic Ocean or the Gulf of Mexico from any of hundreds of small inlets and harbors on the Florida coast and moved by river transport on the St. Johns River north to the other states of the confederacy. Florida was not important militarily however it produced beef cattle, naval stores, lumber and sea salt that were vital to support the Confederate war effort.

At the time of the Civil War, more than 40% of the people in the St. Johns River valley were African, most of the blacks were slaves, there were some free blacks such as members of the Kingsley family who lived in Florida under Spanish rule before the United States acquired Florida in ?1234.

The plantation economy was under great stress because the owners of the plantations were required to serve in the Confederate armed forces. For the plantation owners who stayed at home, because of the blockade, there was no ready, accessible market for the crops. The slaves who relied upon the plantation system for their meager living, had no good options, The Union Forces could not care for all of the refugee slaves. Some of the slaves were recruited into the U.S. Colored Infantry troops.

The Union steam tug USS Columbine, armed with 2 Parrot Rifles and four 20 pounders, arrived at the St. Johns River, in Florida, towing a coal transport vessel in February of 1864. The ship was part of the South Atlantic Blockading Squadron of the United States Navy.

The Columbine joined the ships; U.S.S. Mahaska, Dai Ching, Water Witch, Oleander, Ottawa and Norwich that were stationed at Jacksonville. These ships were assigned to provide transportation and support to the United States Army and to capture or destroy all shipping on the St. Johns River and tributaries.

The U.S. Army under the command of General Seymour. Was retreating back to Jacksonville with more than 1,200 killed or wounded from the battle of Olustee at Ocean Pond near Lake City. The confederate forces were victorious in this battle of Olustee but the fighting had been ferocious and neither side was up to strength.

The Union forces controlled Jacksonville. The navy ships, because of the many small rivers in the Jacksonville area could play a large part in the defense of the city. The Confederate troops had great respect for the cannon fire from the ships. The U.S. Navy controlled the river and the gunboats moved about at will. The Confederate forces harassed the Union navy by setting torpedoes and cannon fire from the shore.

In 1864 communications between people were more or less restricted to letters and orders delivered by courier, visible signals such as flags and signal lamps were used between ships. Electrical telegraph systems were not reliable as cables were cut repeatedly by the locals.

Captured prisoners, freed slaves and local citizens were good sources of information. Ship commanders and field officers were more or less on their own for days with no orders or intelligence reaching them as they carried out their duty. Supply lines were long and frequently interrupted.

The Yankee Forces confiscated all ships, machinery, wood fuel, cotton, corn, rice, naval stores such as turpentine and rosin, salt and salt making equipment that they could find along the river... Exports and imports by the confederates were next to impossible.

The Seminoles, the wandering tribes of Indians and escaped slaves from North and South Carolina driven off their lands by the colonists in the Carolinas, took advantage of the chaos of war and sold cattle to both sides and looted plantations from their villages in central Florida.

On February the Columbine and the Ottowa made a trip to Palatka after ferrying troops to a fort on the river and they burned 6 scows that they found moored at the devil's elbow turn in the river. They delivered mail at Picolata took aboard union refugees who were making their way north. They stopped at # 10 and destroyed a boat, they took 4 bbl of rosin and after leaving the place, and they towed Ottawa across flats at Orange Springs and proceeded to Tocoi and took onboard another family of refugees. They coaled up from Ottawa anchored off black creek. In morning went the Columbine proceeded up Black Creek and destroyed a boat at Taylors Ferry. Questioning refugees they learned of three steamboats up the river. Lt. Commander Breese reported Palatka was nearly destroyed.

In March the Pawnee, the Ottawa and the Mahaska were assigned to duty protecting Jacksonville. The rebels were reported to have a force of 15,000 troops west of Jacksonville. The Columbine

-

brought troops down the river to Jacksonville to add to the fortifications of the city.

The Columbine was sent upriver to the Oklawaha River and beyond looking for the stern wheel confederate steamer reported operating in the area. Ensign Sanborne captured the Confederate General Sumpter Steamer at Lake George with little problem. Sanborne dispatched the prize steamer with a prize crew to capture the Hattie Brock steamer up the river from Lake George. They captured all officers and the crew.

In March, 1864 the Columbine and the Pawnee penetrated 220 miles upriver from Jacksonville and captured 2 steamers with 93 bales cotton. Some of the cotton bales were marked as being produced on Drayton Island by Rembert. They stopped in Lake George and went ashore on Drayton Island to capture John Rembert the son of the owner of the Drayton island Plantation. Both Rembert's were veterans of the Rebel Army. They stopped several times and finally captured young Wm. P. Rembert. Prisoners of the Union or Confederates did not fare well, in Andersonville prison, one of the worst, 35% of the prisoners died each year.

In April 1864, the transport Maple Leaf was blown up by torpedo off Mandarin returning from Palatka and the army transport steamer Hunter was also sunk by a torpedo between Picolata and Jacksonville. These torpedoes were basically wooden barrels of gun powder with a contact fuse that were weighted to float below the surface of the river. A system of ropes would catch on the moving boat and pull the torpedoes into the hull of the ship.

May 21, 1864 Ensign Sanborne left Welaka heading for Jacksonville with the steam tug Columbine side wheeler. He expected to meet the Ottawa at Dunn's Creek, several miles down the river. He had received reports that the rebels were in the woods along the river near Horse Landing and he beat to quarters and had all men stand by for possible fire from the rebels. As he rounded the point he ordered the torpedo catchers lowered and he opened fire on the road and landing with his guns.

He saw nothing of the enemy until suddenly two pieces of artillery, concealed by the undergrowth, opened fire simultaneously. The first shots cut the rudder chains and the pilot left his post a jumped over the side. The Columbine almost immediately went ashore into a mud bank. At the same time a shot had severed the steam pipe that caused the ship to lose the ability to move.

The quarter deck was swept by rebel fire and it became obvious that he would be unable to repel the attack. He called his officers together and they agreed to surrender. During the lull in fighting he met with the rebel officers and they agreed to terms of surrender. More than 16 sailors were killed and many injured. Many black soldiers attempted to swim across the river with unknown results.

The rebel commander set fire to the prize ship to prevent the possible recapture by the Union troops. This action was one of the few times that a navy ship was destroyed by an artillery battery

Chapter 11   Zephaniah Kingsley

The United States gained possession of Florida from Spain in the year 1819, and made it a territory of the United States in 1822; Zephaniah Kingsley filed claims of ownership to many parcels of land in East Florida, primarily along the St. Johns River. Drayton Island was among the parcels. The purpose was to convert his Spanish land titles into marketable United States titles. To further his interest, he became an elected official of the Florida territorial Government in 1823. Despite many obstacles, he managed to have most of his claims approved by 1827.

Kingsley found that the intent of the Territorial Government was to pass strict laws that would support the property rights of the slave holders in their slaves and to severely punish anyone who took any action that would tend to be in opposition to slavery.

Florida had been a haven for runaway slaves and Indians from the original 13 colonies. Zephaniah Kingsley found that some of his own actions such as giving slaves their freedom would cause him to be arrested. Kingsley was considered an enlightened slaveholder and he had many multiracial children with several black wives. Kingsley considered being a slave was a condition not related to race.

The new laws would reinstate the condition of slavery to anyone who had ever been a slave or was the child of someone who had ever been a slave. These laws were so onerous to his family that he left

Florida and purchased a Plantation in Haiti. Zephaniah transferred the ownership of Drayton Island and some other properties to George Kingsley, his brother in 1836. Zephaniah died in 1842. George Kingsley was killed in a shipwreck in 1846.

Chapter 12 Island Owners

My research indicates that prior to the voyages of European based people such as Leif Erickson and Columbus, there is no doubt that people lived in the Americas for many thousands of years. These people were named Indians by someone and the name hides the varied cultures of the tribes. I suspect that the history of these people, before the Europeans arrived, is as interesting as the history after. This book is silent about these early people. They were the first owners of Drayton Island.

During the first Spanish period of 1492-1763 I have found no record of ownership of Drayton Island however it probably was included in some land grant of many thousands of acres. When you think about it, why try to establish a plantation in the wilderness and fight Indians for the land when land was available close in to St. Augustine with the protection of the soldiers at the fort? As far as I know, the Indians were the only settlers on the Drayton Island during this period however it is always possible that other people lived on the island without leaving any sign of their presence.

During the British period, 1763-1783 Drayton Island was granted to William Drayton but as far as I know, no major work or building was accomplished on the Island. Drayton was noted for his non-interest in the properties he acquired while serving as Chief Justice of East Florida.

During the second Spanish period, 1783-1819 the previous British grants were extinguished and new Spanish grants were made to people who met the Spanish criteria. At the end of the period, Zephaniah Kingsley owned Drayton Island and several other parcels of land along the St. Johns River.

When Florida became a territory of the United States in 1819 the territorial government ratified some of the old Spanish grants and Zephaniah Kingsley seemed to make a business of ratifying his claims. He was elected to the territorial government and had many of his claims ratified. Kingsley established a plantation on Drayton Island and located part of his family there to oversee the operation of a citrus nursery.

Kingsley was disappointed in the territorial laws regarding slavery and race. The laws passed were so onerous that Kingsley deeded all his property in Florida to his brother, George, and Zephaniah Kingsley moved most of his family to Jamaica and established a plantation. Later,

George Kingsley was killed in a shipwreck and the property passed to his estate.

John C. Calhoun Jr. purchased Drayton Island or Anzie Island as it was called at that time, in April of 1855 from the estate of George Kingsley, Zephaniah Kingsley's brother. It is my impression that there were few improvements on Drayton Island at that time although Kingsley had cleared some land and established orange groves. In December of 1855,

Anzie Island was auctioned in order to pay John Calhoun Jr. creditors. Duff Green, for reasons unknown, purchased Anzie Island at the auction. Duff Green sold the island to William P. Rembert in March of 1859. Rembert was the last person to own all of Drayton Island. Rembert was a plantation owner from South Carolina; he brought his slaves to Drayton Island, and established a plantation that produced cotton and other farm products.

Rembert had less than five years on the Island because the Civil War occurred and owning slaves became illegal in the United States. Most of the Rembert period of ownership was during the war. Union navy ships controlled the river and all goods potentially useful to the Confederate cause were confiscated. Rembert's son, a member of the Confederate army was captured on the island by the Union navy.

When the war was over, Rembert began to sell parts of the island. The first sale was in 1872 to a Mr. Wright and his wife Flora who was a member of the women's sufferance group; they purchased 400 some acres on the southwest end of the island for a farm. Mr. Wright's brother had a farm on the mainland in Georgetown.

The second sale war to Richard Towle in 1875 who created the Towle subdivision on the Southeast shore, 30 some lots 10 chains wide, (165 feet), and about 1500 feet deep. These lots were part of a scheme to sell lots to hotel guests that stayed in the new hotel located on lots 6&7. In 1878 the hotel lots were sold for taxes and the hotel was no longer there. I assume it burned.

All of the above was possible because the steamboats opened the river to tourists from the north and provided transportation of produce from the south to the north. Many of the tourists were seeking a warm climate for medical reasons.

Rembert made more sales of property on the island until his death in 1877. He is buried in the cemetery at the end of Drayton Island ferry Road in Georgetown.

Chapter 13 Quercus Virginiana a trip on the St Johns River in 1878

There are silent living participants and witnesses to the history of Drayton Island, some dating back to before Columbus. They stand near the shoreline of the great lake. Live oak trees, Quercus Virginiana, some with trunks more than 10 feet in diameter, mark the location of long forgotten dwellings and abandoned sand roads. In summer, under the shade of the massive branches, tinged green with small waxy leaves and maturing acorns any person, in any age, would enjoy the light breezes off the lake that move the gray, sometimes green, Spanish moss in a never ending swaying dance. Old fallen branches provided a place to sit and find a moment of peace. It is cooler under the canopy and only grasses grow in the deep shade.

Long forgotten wooden houses were built under or near these trees, during the 500 years since Columbus, by people that made Drayton Island their home for part of their lives. The wooden houses vanished without a trace, even the brick foundations would be salvaged in a land of sand. Some houses built in the 1900's and well maintained and modernized by their owners are standing along the lakefront. I do not know of any existing buildings on the island that predate the civil war.

The island was on the Indian frontier during the two Spanish periods and during the intervening British period. The Civil War and the end of slavery ended the plantation period along the river. The short steamboat era ended with the extension of the railroad to south Florida. Hard freezes in the 1890's drove the citrus industry south. The peak population of about 150 occurred after the Civil War during the Steamboat era when transportation of tourists in and farm produce out on riverboats was inexpensive and profitable.

All of the constantly changing conditions above prevented or discouraged families from putting down roots and making improvements that were lasting. Without a long period of predictable economic conditions and a system of laws that guarantee property ownership rights there is no incentive to improve the land and buildings. Capital for expansion and improvements is accumulated slowly. Knowledge of farming and establishment of markets is also a slow process in a time when communications were rudimentary and trading was a man to man process where character and trust were essential.

The Indians, slaves, indentured servants and paid overseers had no capital and no property ownership rights. The land grants by the far off crown were in many cases given to royalty that had no interest in either the land or the workers. The last two owners, Kingsley and Rembert were farmers trying to carry on the plantation system that was built upon slaves and indentured workers. Kingsley, who had mixed race children, was unable to live with the racial laws of the Florida Territory and he moved to Jamaica. Rembert only owned the island for five years or so and the Civil War interfered with three or more years of his tenure. His slaves were freed and he sold parts of the island to land speculators, a hotel was built and burned in three years time. The steamboat era ended and the population moved away.

Quercus Virginiana, witness to 500 years of history is silent.

July, 1878: Martin lived on Drayton Island with his wife and children in a waterfront, rambling frame house shaded by a giant live oak tree covered with Spanish moss. There were seven houses on the southeast side of the island; all were within half a mile of the Drayton Island hotel. In the fall and winter seasons Martin made his living as a fishing and hunting guide catering to northern visitors staying at the hotel.

In the summer, when the hotel was closed, he found occasional carpenter jobs in the area and he maintained his orange grove, boats and equipment. There were about twelve houses on the island and hundreds of acres of farmland, but in the summer, many times, he and his family and a few neighbors were the only people on the island at night. Most of the farmers and workers preferred to live on the mainland in Georgetown across the river.

Tonight his wife's sister, Catherine, who lived in Georgetown across the river, was staying with them, helping out, because two of the children were sick.

Martin stepped out onto the front porch and closed the screened door behind him. The faint light of the mantelpiece coal oil lamp could be seen through the door screen and the living room window. On the porch, Martin put on his boots, and waited for his eyes to adjust to the darkness. He carried his lantern down the steps to the cement sidewalk that led from the house to the dock.

Martin could still see the lake and his long wooden dock in the dim light of late evening. Several storms with thunder and flashing lightning were working their way across the south end of the lake. The last light outlined the dark line of clouds on the western horizon.

Martin's long wooden dock extended almost 700 feet across the shallow weed-beds that flanked the south-east Shore of Drayton Island. About 150 feet out from the shore Martin had built a shed on cedar pilings to house his equipment and traps that were used during the eel season in the fall and winter. The smoked eel season brought in a serious amount of money and helped to support the family. In the cool of the winter, smoked eels would keep on the long rail journey from Huntington Station, near Georgetown, to the Grampp Bar on the waterfront of Elizabeth port in N.J.

At the end of the dock, Martin had built a large boathouse to keep the rain and the weather from the steam powered launch he used on his guide trips to his special hunting and fishing grounds. Wealthy, northern clients had advanced him money to build the dock and to maintain his fleet of rowboats, the houseboat he called "Duke" and the steam launch that allowed him to take his friends and clients on the hunting and fishing trips.

The launch in the boathouse, and the boxy houseboat named the Duke that was tied up alongside were both constructed of live oak and pine cut from local logs in the Georgetown sawmill across the river. They were simple boats built and designed for the shallow lake by Martin and other local carpenters. The launch was powered by a steam engine. The boiler could be fired by wood, coal or kerosene. The side mounted helm wheel was connected to the rudder with a sash chain that ran through holes in the ribs to a rudder bar on the rear deck.

The steam launch was undergoing a seasonal overhaul and was out of commission. Martin stopped about halfway out to the end of the dock, at the steps that led to a water level platform with a row boat tethered to the pilings. He descended the stairs and pulled the rowboat in to the platform. The faint light from his lantern probed the rowboat for snakes that sometimes climbed into the boat. He was afraid of the arrogant cottonmouth snakes that were aggressive and deadly.

The blended sound of insects, frogs and other creatures filled the air over the shallow water weed beds. Martin stepped down onto the main seat of the rowboat; he turned to face the stern and slowly sat down in the rowing position, easing his feet under the rear seat. He placed the oars into the locks and untied the rope that secured the rowboat to the dock.

Martin rowed the boat along the dock, heading for the coffee colored tannin stained waters of the lake out past the sand bar. He lightly dipped the oars into the matted weeds and urged the boat forward through the thick growth of floating water hyacinths, spatterdock, water lilies, and coon tail that grew in the shallow water by the dock.

The sun had set and it was now completely dark except for the faint light from the stars that peeked through the clouds occasionally. The dim light made it possible to see whitecaps on the waves out on the lake. Martin rowed out the channel through the weeds he maintained from the sand-bar into the boathouse.

The night noises were louder than ever as he rowed through the heart of the weeds. Clouds of blind mosquitoes, that were really midges, and harmless, surrounded him with their buzz.

Several water birds squawked their disapproval of Martin and his boat. He could not see them. But he could image the herons opening their wings, lifting their feet and gliding off into the darkness.

The alligators that lived in the shallows were not spooked by a row boat and would move out and stay just ahead of the slow craft.

The symphony of noise from the insect creatures took on a tempo of rising and falling volume as if a conductor was leading an orchestra. The insect symphony was drowned out by the frogs. There were thousands of frogs and toads that lived in the weed beds, much to the delight of the bass and garfish.

The breeze from the southwest was increasing by the time Martin reached the deeper water of the lake and it was raising a light chop along the sand bar and causing much larger waves to build up further out in the lake.

His rowboat was able to cope with the choppy water with no problems. From the open water outside the weed-beds, looking left, northeast down the island, he could see the dim glow of the navigation beacon that marked the north end of Lake George and the beginning of the St. Johns River to the north.

As he pulled on the oars, Martin settled down into a rhythm that he could sustain for several hours. He pulled on the oars with a moderate force. He rocked forward and back on each stroke and made tiny corrections to direct the course. The eight houses he passed along the shore of the island were dark. The hotel was shuttered for the summer.

The Rembert house, the family that had owned Drayton Island, during the Civil War was also dark; the Rembert family was visiting kin in South Carolina.

By the time he passed the beacon light at the north end of the lake, the breeze preceding the weather front was becoming a wind and light rain was falling. Almost all light was gone now that the clouds had covered the sky. The wind was with him and it helped him as he worked his way up the channel between Georgetown and the Island. As he rowed past the black settlement he could see figures gathered around an open barbeque fire.

Crossing the lake from Drayton Island to the western mainland on the way to Fort Gates would be the hardest part of the journey. The long fetch of water between the northwest mainland and Drayton Island would be rough. The wind was driving the waves up the three channels around Hog Island and Drayton Island. The waves would meet north of Drayton Island and he would be in the middle of the resulting turmoil.

The stern of the handmade rowboat was built with a wide wooden seat that was useful while pulling fish and crab traps and nets but it could also allow an overtaking wave to fill the boat The back and sides of the boat hull did not extend above the seat. Tonight was going to be a test of the boat and the man.

-

Martin braced his boots against the seat supports and the ribs of the boat. The oars were fitted with leather collars that fit into the horns of the brass oarlocks. The small boat was designed for lake not ocean waves.

As he rounded the point at the north end of the island, near the Indian shell mounds, the waves became larger and disorganized. The bow of the rowboat was lighter than the stern and rose up over the oncoming waves in a sprightly manner. The course heading required for this journey was in the direction of the waves. As Martin rowed the boat out past the north end of the island, he timed his oar stokes so that he was able to pull the stern of the boat out from under the steep following wave.

In the darkness he could not see far. Occasionally, a wave greater than the average would loom up behind the boat and he would have to pull the oars hard to prevent the wave from overtopping the stern... One wave over the stern would change the weight balance and allow subsequent waves to crash into the boat.

The challenge of rowing the boat through these waves lightened Martin's mood. Bending forward and pulling back with each oar stroke was a strain on his hands, arms and shoulders. His boots were wedged against the boat ribs. The combined effort of all parts of his body was required to maintain his seat and provide the power to prevent the swamping of his boat by the following waves. Despite his light mood, he was slowly using up his strength. He was happy to cross the sandbar at Black Point and leave the large waves behind him in the channel.

Under the overhanging trees he pulled the rowboat up against the bank to rest. He could not wait to stand up and move about to ease his muscle pain. Martin cut the top off of one of his oranges and cut down around through the sections with his pocket knife to release the juice, he sucked the juice out of the orange just as he had when he was a kid.

He was not alone on this section of the shore. All of the blind mosquitoes hatched tonight between Drayton Island and Hog Island had blown ashore, they filled the air and covered the trees. Tonight they were exceptionally thick. Martin knew that they would not hurt him, but he also knew that they would be in his eyes, his mouth, and his ears and inside his shirt and probably in his boots. As he pushed the boat back out onto the lake, he spit and blew his nose several times.

He continued along the shore of the mainland sometimes under the branches of trees, always well within sight of land, the wind helped push the boat. Slow and steady he moved along the shore until he reached the ornate boathouse at Fort Gates.

He tied his boat at the dock and started to walk up the long sidewalk to the house. The wind was still blowing up a storm out in the river and scattered raindrops splashed on the dock. The house was dark and shuttered for the summer season. The caretaker lived in the rear caretaker quarters.

Martin climbed the steps to the kitchen door. He knocked and shouted "Hey, George", several times before he heard an answer from inside the house. George and his companion, Sara, lived in the house all summer. They took care of the yard and maintained the house for the New York shipping magnate owner.

Through the frosted glass in the door, the darkness inside the house was broken by the rays of a weak light. A striking match lit an oil lamp and George carried the lamp to the table. "Who is it?" asked George as he walked to the door. "Martin", George opened the door and invited Martin in to the kitchen.

Martin stepped out of his boots and entered the kitchen, "George, I am looking for Doctor Cane, Booty told me that he was here taking care of Sara. My son Lincoln is sick, he has trouble breathing, he has a fever, and we have tried everything."

Slowly, Martin realized that George did not have good news for him. George had a concerned look on his face, serious. Martin slowly sat down in the chair at the kitchen table.

George walked over to Martin and put his hand on his shoulder, "I am sorry to tell you that Dr. Cane and Sara both left on the boat for Palatka this afternoon, she was going to her sisters and Dr, Cane was going to Palatka on some business. As George spoke, Martin realized that it might be several days until a doctor could be found.

The heavy large raindrops began to roar on the tin roof of the kitchen. George opened the firebox door of the ornate porcelain kitchen wood stove and threw in a handful of fat wood splits and some oak kindling. He filled the coffee pot at the kitchen pitcher pump with rain water from the cistern and put it on the stove. He sat across from Martin at the table. "You better stay here till the storm is over." Martin looked stricken.

A sudden, even stronger gust of wind shook the sturdy house; the chimney howled with the sudden wind, a bright flash of lightning starkly lit the room. A loud blast of thunder shook the house and rolled down the St. Johns River Valley toward Drayton Island.

Martin wanted to cry out in rage against the sickness that was ruining his life. His only son, Lincoln, had the disease. He had seen others die of the disease but he was not ready to see Lincoln die of the disease. He had to do something.

Martin turned to George and began to talk while banging his fist down on the table. "George, we have to do something. We have to get old Doc Cane back to the Island before morning; I know he can save Lincoln."

Martin continued his entreaty to George, "We could fire up the boss's boat and go to Palatka and bring him back before noon tomorrow, maybe a lot before noon." It is only 7 miles to Welaka, about 7 more miles to Horse Landing, about 7 more miles to Edgewater, and about 7 more miles to Palatka. The boss's boat runs 7 miles an hour we could be there in 4 hours. I know every sandbar and beacon light from here to there."

George and Martin sat silently across from each other at the kitchen table and drank their coffee with evaporated milk and the boss's sugar. Finally George banged his fist on the table and said, "Let's go." Let's run that mahogany beauty up to Palatka and give old Doc Cane the ride of his life." Martin stood up and smiled a thank you to George.

The boathouse at Fort gates, like the main house and the clubhouse with the bowling alley. Was built from the best material by expert carpenters and designed by a New York architectural design firm that only did it right. In the boathouse the sleek mahogany steam runabout was tied in its stall like a racehorse. She was an open boat with a canopy with the boiler and engine mounted amidships.

George, as caretaker of the Fort gates complex had the keys to everything and he had some experience operating the mahogany beauty. Martin was the river pilot and knew the river, and he knew about the kerosene fired boiler of this boat.

The boys needed a little luck to make this trip successfully and those things were a break in the weather, no fog, and a little luck getting the boiler fired up. The kerosene mantle lantern made it possible to see in the darkness of the boat house. George and martin busied themselves getting the boiler fired up and checking out the engine.

It took about a half an hour to get the boiler up to pressure; they had filled the boat house with smoke and the smell of kerosene. They cast off the ropes and eased the engine into forward. Martin took the helm and George fussed with the boiler as they started out into the river heading north.

-

The river north of Fort Gates opened into a section that was about half a mile wide, there were no houses along this part of the river on either shore, black on black with black water and black skies.

George and Martin eased along through the rain at half speed staring ahead hoping to see something that would give them a clue where they were. The storm was almost over now and the wind from the southwest would soon bring clearing skies and increased visibility.

They could sense that they were paralleling the wooded shoreline. They would steer left until they could sense the forest or see the tips of the eel grass showing at the water surface. After about one hour of the slow progress, they believed that they had entered Little Lake George.

Martin decided to cross Little Lake George on a due North course and search for the lights of Welaka after they got about halfway across. The rain and wind were settling down and the skies were lighter after the storm. They could see further out ahead of them now. George stood up and shouted to Martin, "Something is wrong, I do not know what but I see something in the water and a faint light."

Martin slowed the engine and stood up to look where George was pointing. He could see a weak lantern far off in the distance and something in the water ahead of his boat. Martin thought, I think I see someone walking on the water!

George shut down the steam to the engine, the boat slowed in the water and they sat and listened as the boat drifted. George raised the galvanized funnel, puckered his lips like a bugler and blew a long trumpet blast. As George and Martin listened the boat bumped into something solid. They both knew that they had bumped into a log. As they looked about them they saw many logs, big logs, lying in the water with only a small portion above the water.

They were in the middle of a log rafting operation that had gone bad. Far up the Oklawaha River the logging crew had assembled a series of log rafts that would be floated down the Oklawaha to the St. Johns. Halfway down, around Orange Springs Landing storm water crested and the crew lost control of the rafts and they jammed the river channel on a serpentine curve.

The rafting crew decided to break up the rafts and let the logs find their way to the St. Johns where they would be collected and rafted down the river to the Cypress sawmill in Palatka. The faint light they had seen was a lantern on the pull boat owned by Jumbos Cypress Contractor.

They heard an answering trumpet and someone called a rebel yell from the pull boat. George answered the rebel yell and began to paddle the mahogany boat towards the faint light. As they worked their way through the floating logs, rowing and polling their way around the scattered cypress logs, they got closer and closer to the faint light.

The Jumbos cypress company floating logging camp comprising three barges took shape as they approached. One barge was a two story bunk house, another barge was the cookhouse and mess hall and the third barge was an equipment warehouse and shop. The pull boat was tied up to the barges.

Answering a "hey", Martin and George made their way over to the pull boat and tied the mahogany beauty to the cleat. "You fellows sure have the river blocked with these logs" remarked George to the deckhand who walked over to lean on the rail. The deckhand joked, " If we knew you were coming we would have cleared this river for you."

Martin asked the deckhand, "How is the best way to get around this mess and go on to Palatka?" "Well Sir, if you go to the east shore by Welaka you can be pretty sure there are none of our logs over that way. We are making up a boom to round up these logs at first light and pull them into muddy cove."

"Say, what is your name? I think I know you!" asked Martin of the deckhand. "Taylor Douglas" answered the deckhand. "Did you ever work in the Georgetown Sawmill?" asked Martin. "Sure did". "I am Martin from Drayton Island and this is George from Fort Gates, we are heading to Palatka tonight and we want to get going."

"I remember you, Martin; you sorted through all of the boards picking out the best ones for your boats. You sure made a mess of my neat piles. Good to see you and have a safe trip."

Martin and George worked their way eastward, poling and paddling the boat toward the Welaka shore and when they were pretty sure they were free of the logs they started the engine and headed for the dim lights of Welaka.

"That Taylor Douglas was in the 33rd Infantry of the Colored Regiment." Martin told George, "He was on the Columbine when she was captured by Colonel Dickinson. He dove off and hid in the swamps."

George asked Martin, "Did you ever go aboard that floating logging camp?"No." "It is no Sunday School picnic. The bunks are three high and each bunk holds three men. They give the workers 10 minutes to eat supper and everyone craps in the river. It is better than a turpentine camp but not much"

"The saw shop is run by a German guy and he runs a tight ship. There are two benches for sharpening and setting the saws. There is a forge to repair most anything. They probably have a hundred saws and axes in that shop and two men work all day to keep them in shape. The white guys sleep and eat in the end of the shop barge."

They started the engine after they were free of the floating logs and headed for the lights of Welaka. The high shell banks of the river at Welaka were a contrast to most of the river banks of the St. Johns River. Welaka was located high up on the bank and the riverboat landing was at least thirty feet below the main street reached by several sections of stairs clinging to the hillside and a narrow road that ran along the river to a point where the bank was lower. The teamster's freight and passenger wagons used this road when meeting the riverboats.

Martin and George decided to stop at the landing to get some fuel for the boat and a bottle from Snow. Snow was as black as you could get, he was almost purple but his big smile of white teeth made him a favorite with all of the passengers. At this time of the year the hotel and boarding houses were practically empty of guests. It seemed Snow was always at the landing, day and night.

They sent a boy that was night fishing for catfish to find Snow and George stayed with the boat as Martin climbed the stairs to Main Street. Martin expected to find the store closed but he knew where the owner lived. They wanted to get a five gallon can of kerosene as a backup supply of fuel for the boat.

Martin met Snow on the way to the Welaka Store on the sand street that ran under the huge old live oak trees that thrived on the high banks of the river. Snow was carrying a burlap sack and Martin could hear the muffled clink of bottle against bottle. Martin gave Snow the money and took the bag of bottles from him. Martin figured it was four bottles of wine but Snow looked at him with a polite stare and said "whiskey"

Snow asked Martin "where are you going? Martin said, ,"To find the storekeeper for some coal oil"

Snow followed up with, "but where are you going?"

Martin looked at Snow's purple-black face and answered him as straight as he could, "We are going to Palatka tonight."

"Got room for a passenger?' Snow asked.

"If it is a friend of yours, yes." Answered Martin. "But we are leaving now"

Snow stood in the road next to Martin surrounded by the night, the live oaks and there were no lights in the few houses, only the far off barking of a dog Snow said, "I will get the kerosene, you go back to the boat and my friend will join you shortly."

Martin carried the bag of bottles down the haul road to the river and put the bottles into the boat. George was slouched back on the seat and snoozing. Martin got on the boat and busied himself getting familiar with the bottles.

They heard someone coming and as the person approached they got the impression of a large man carrying a can of oil. He arrived at the boat and lifted the oil over the side. "Hi, I am Buck, Snow sent me, and I have to go to Palatka, tonight."

Martin and George both knew Buck; they had worked with him here and there for many years. Buck was a hard worker and many times he worked as the lead man or the boss of a crew. He ruled with an iron hand and would fight in a minute.

Buck had several women on the string and many children called him Daddy. Buck was a joker and his favorite was to come up to the steamboat landing when some stuffy white man was getting off the boat and he would shout across the crowd and wave, "Hello Daddy!"

Buck said to George and Martin, "Don't ask me any questions because you do not want to know where I am going or where I've been."

The three men shoved off the river bank and the steam launch headed north on the river out of Welaka. The night was dark but somehow they could see pretty well across the river and there were beacons up along the river channel.

"We sank the COLUMBINE right here", George said, pointing at Horse Landing. Captain Dickison cavalry and artillery made history right here."

Martin was silent. He thought about the loss of the crew and troops in that battle between the Yankee ship Columbine and the Confederate artillery.

-

Many Union Navy men were killed or captured and many enlisted colored troops were killed or captured. The ship burned after a lucky artillery shot carried away the rudder chains.

Martin said to George, "You Rebs had one Lucky shot" George was silent.

They decided to have a drink on the war and they passed the bottle around. George had a glass fruit jar stored aboard the boat just for this purpose. He reached over the side and filled the glass with river water and poured in a couple of fingers of whiskey. Martin and Buck drank from the bottle.

As they reached the Islands around the entrance to Dunn's Creek the skies opened up and it rained buckets. Terrible lightning lit the black clouds and the tall trees on the Islands.

Martin steered the boat from one side of the river to the other as they passed down the crooked river. The sand bars hugged the inside of the curves and the channel was on the outside of the curves in most cases.

The storm faded and the first sign of dawn was the brightening of the scene. They passed San Mateo and they could see Harts Grove in the distance. It seemed as though the river ended at this point but the river doubled back around Devils Elbow into the wide river at Palatka.

Martin estimated a four hour trip but they had taken eight hours to make the trip. They were working on the second bottle of Snow's special and were in a good mood. Martin, after the trip and the whiskey, was feeling better about his son's illness; after all, his wife and his sister in law were both smart people and could handle the situation.

They landed in Palatka on an old unused pier and Buck left the group. He was headed north out of Florida because the Sheriff was out to arrest him for stealing a pig. Buck denied stealing the pig but the Kangaroo court in Putnam County was not set up for a vigorous defense of a poor black man.

George would stay with the boat and see to the repairs before returning home. Martin would find Doctor Cane; convince him to come back to Drayton Island on the riverboat named Welaka that left a ten in the morning. Buck would merge with the fireman crew of the next boat to Jacksonville, Savannah or Charleston.

Martin searched all of the big hotels for Doctor Cane and had no luck. Whatever business Dr. Cane was taking care of he maintained a low profile. Deciding it was impossible to find the doctor, Martin walked to the pier where the Welaka was loading and unloading freight.

Teamsters with freight wagons were at the dock picking up the freight. The two horse teams, with oat bags on their noses, munched oats contentedly as they waited for the wagons to be loaded. The odor of horse manure and urine, wood smoke and turpentine filled the warm air.

The Palatka harbor was surrounded with wooden piers, the sawmill and anchored ships. Hotels looked out over the waterfront and the ferry to Hubbard Hart's East Palatka paddled its way across the river.

Martin found a shady place to rest and he napped until time for the Welaka to shove off. Martin and the Captain of the Welaka went way back and Martin could ride free but the Captain did not want him in the pilot house.

The covered "around the boat" observation walk on the passenger deck of the steamboat Welaka was interrupted by the paddlewheel housings on both sides of the ship. Passengers could walk from the bow to the stern section through the interior passageway between the great wheels. The passenger deck included tiny cabins, and bow and stern decks.

The deck above the passenger deck contained the pilot house with crew quarters and lifeboats. The smokestack from the boiler belched black smoke that sometimes blew down at the passengers. The captain would change course if he could.

The lower deck was the machinery, fuel, and freight deck. The floor of this deck was made of strong cypress boards and was designed to carry the weight of the freight and the fuel such as coal or wood. The machinery consisted of three major systems, the boiler where fuel was burned to produce steam, and two steam engines each of which drove one paddle wheel.

The engines could be run in forward or reverse and the side wheels could be disconnected from the engines with a clutch. As the boat traveled narrow winding streams, control of the boat could be obtained by reversing one wheel while the other was in forward.

There were several steam powered pumps to provide makeup water to the boiler and to supply the water cooling to the engines. The fuel was pine logs cut into four foot long pieces. The firemen could throw these logs into the firebox with great accuracy.

The freight deck was stacked with freight. A casual observer could identify many wooden barrels that might contain oranges, orange juice, resin, turpentine, fish, produce, rice, etc. Bales of cotton, boxes of clothing, shook for boxes and barrels, livestock in a pen, plows and wagons, furniture, lumber, bricks and everything else might be seen.

The men that fired the engines and worked the freight had steel wheeled hand trucks to move the freight as quickly as possible. At every stop time was money. Most stops on the river had a dock with steel rails and a hand pushed cart to handle the freight from the boat to the shore. Some docks had a freight building at the end so that freight could be accumulated.

Show mileage and stops

The Tecumseh steamed up the river into Little Lake George after the Welaka stop. Martin was standing in the bow of the freight deck enjoying the breeze. As he looked out across the expanse of water he could see several boats of fishermen near the Croaker Hole spring in the north end of the lake casting for shrimp. And a few boats around the mouth of the Oklawaha River that appeared to be searching for logs. As the Tecumseh entered the river flanked by pinewoods, in the distance, miles away, he saw a column of black smoke rising above the trees. It was not a forest fire smoke with a broad base; it was a spot source smoke that might occur from a boat or building fire or perhaps a huge pile of logs. Martin knew it was a fire on the Island and it must be a building.

The ship passed Fort gates without making a stop and headed for Georgetown, the next scheduled stop to drop off the mail. Martin wanted to get home and he would pick up his rowboat some other time.

Martin had been concerned about his sick son Lincoln and his failed effort to find a doctor, the column of black smoke now gave him another worry. What was burning? He thought of all of the houses, including his. He thought of the hotel, not so much of the building but the end of his sportsmen guiding business that relied on the hotel guests.

At the Georgetown landing there were quite a few people standing around talking about the fire. It was the hotel and it had been burning all morning. Quite a few boats had crossed to the island and people were carrying furniture and hotel goods out of the hotel and the lawn was covered with beds, bureaus, chairs, tables, linens and miscellaneous stuff that could be removed before the fire reached the lower stories. Lightning during the night must have struck a chimney and started a long smoldering fire up on the third floor.

The captain of the Tecumseh decided not to make a stop at the Drayton Island wharf house, a steamboat landing built out in the lake, way out past the weed beds in deeper water to serve the hotel guests. He did not have any freight or passengers except Martin who was a non-paying free loader and the mail that he could leave in Georgetown. He had received word that the wharf house was surrounded by boats and it would be impossible to safely bring the Tecumseh into the pier.

Martin's son Lincoln lies under a Quercus Virginiana near the hotel site on Drayton Island. Martin, his wife, George, the Tecumseh Captain, Snow and all of the people that carried out the furniture lie under a Quercus Virginiana somewhere in Putnam County, near the river.

Quercus Virginiana, witness to 500 years of history is silent.

-

Chapter 14: A visit to Drayton Island ca1850

Authors Note: In the winter of 1851 a party of Northerners visited Drayton Island traveling from St. Augustine to the St. Johns River and traveling up the river to Drayton Island. At the time, Drayton Island was owned by Zephaniah Kingsley. Kingsley had begun a plantation on the island to raise citrus fruit trees and for other purposes. He owned many parcels of real estate along the St. Johns River and had several wives. His mixed race families were spread out through the river valley. The family on Drayton Island was probably one of his family groups. He was unhappy with the laws that were established in the new Florida Territory as they related to slavery. The harsh laws declared that if a child had one drop of slave blood they would be a slave forever. The following book will give you a look at one point of view. Their trip included a visit to Salt Springs a few miles from Drayton Island. They had provisions for a week.

The following is quoted from the Google Books,

"The Planter 15 years in the south"

BOATING PARTY. Ca 1850

It was on an early day of the February of that remarkably delightful sunny winter which followed the mysterious shower of blazing meteors; when three gentlemen left St. Augustine for the St. John's River, with the exciting object of making a boat voyage up the stream to Drayton Island, in Lake George.

The morning ride from the ancient city to the noble river was through sixteen miles of an atmosphere, resonant of vernal music, and perfumed by myriads of flowers, whose coral lips were rapidly opening to the genial sun. A happier little party has rarely passed over that quiet, and almost desert,—not long after made unquiet by the rifle crack of the Indian; and its sand and its flowers stained with the blood of inoffensive travelers, and of its few peaceful inhabitants. Then,—till decoyed into the death-snare by the assurance of peace, when there was no peace,—the cheerful and happy Weedman;—what passer across that plain ever found, anywhere, more cordial hospitality, than with him and his primitively simple family? Who ever saw anything in Weedman, or in any one of his Germano-Spanish family, but the most delightful simplicity of goodness? Who ever saw anything more simply beautiful and picturesque, than that almost immensity of a man—the ever cheerful and loving father, and gentle master, leading afield, or to the cowmen, his numerous happy sons and daughters, and two or three laughing Negroes? I never did. But, alas! insatiate war gave that peaceful man, and a portion of his family to the Indian tomahawk; and broke up that happy home, where the weary and the benighted traveler had ever found kind and generous hospitality; and where dwellers in the man-made town were wont to visit, to be refreshed by a draught of nature, where

"God made the country."

Should these lines fall under the eye of any survivor of that long gratefully remembered family, let them be accepted as a trifling tribute due to the memory of the murdered father, whom the author esteemed as one of the best and kindest of men; and also as a cordial thank offering to his household for the many pleasant hours enjoyed among them, in their once cheerfully simple, and therefore happy home, untimely desolated. To others, who have never heard of the Weedmans, nor of their humble home on the Picolata road, far away from the haunts of men, I have only to say, pardon this little detour to drop a tear of memory on the bloody grave of an honest man, a noble work of God;—happy in himself,— happy in his family,—happy in love to his God, and to his kind;—nor less happy in being the master of a few faithful slaves, whose pleasures were not a paradox.

Of the three gentlemen, with their small crew of black boatmen,—one a dweller in the land of flowers, was the patron, who generously provided the pleasure; one was "the Doctor," who had been in the South but a few weeks; and the third a sojourner of several months.

The Doctor had visited the South imbued with a northern notion that all the slaves were determinedly biding their time, for any—even the most desperate— chance to free themselves from their condition. Haunted by this absurd notion, and seeing ourselves outnumbered by the slaves, who, as he probably supposed, were only making believe happy and joyous, he secretly expressed some alarm of peril from them, when we might be far

And we rode on quietly, to the tranquil shore, where two years after I "saw another sight." But let not the tranquil present be disturbed by the future trump of war.

With our fine, roomy and staunch boat, well stowed and stored for a week's voyage, we launched out upon the young Flood. As to a Naiad, or genial fairy Water Sprite, come to their aid, the Negroes gave her a melodious song of grateful welcome. In the song, which was anything but classical, save only in the association, there was nothing like an allusion to the mythological water nymph; which, perhaps, as in their capacity of boatmen, they may have heard her often spoken of by classical passengers, was the more remarkable. It was doubtless a mere natural coincidence. Nature is Nature everywhere; and the free imagination, — there is none freer than the southern slave's—is ever employed in the poetical work of personifying her works and wonders; not the least striking of which are the tides of her many waters.

After a few hours made easy by her efficient help, we met the retiring tide on. the current, when more power was required at the oars. The Negroes perspired freely; and our sympathies suggested a landing on an umbrageous and flowery bank, enriched by a native orange grove, in both fruit and blossom. There our watermen, as handy as happy, spread our cloth for dinner, on a gorgeous carpet of the little red lily, and the creeping sensitive plant; in the deep shade of a large magnolia, where the golden fruit would hang over our heads.

The Dr., who had looked to see the men lie down in the shade, to rest their tired limbs, was delighted to find them apparently far less weary than their passengers, and with mirth and high relish, enjoying the much praised refreshment which had been so liberally provided.

On the second day, having been rather disturbed through much of the night, by their songs and laughter around their blazing fire, our sympathies for their toil at the oars was not particularly painful. Indeed every night they seemed by no means as weary as we were; and during the whole excursion, they manifestly enjoyed it as though it had been entered upon and prosecuted for their special gratification. It gave us pleasure, to the full amount of our capacity for enjoyment, but, with all our supposed advantages, the much greater amount of real pleasure very plainly fell to their lot. Compensate him for the loss of his eyes. By the way, I wonder if Horace was not the better poet—the best of his age in my opinion—for his slave blood? To become such a poet, I would have the metaphorical chain fastened on my limbs to-morrow; as I would give my eyes to be able to create another Paradise Lost."

What most surprised us in the Negroes,—strangers till then to their peculiarities—was their remarkable talent of improvisation. Their extemporaneous songs at the oar, suited to various scenes and occasions and circumstances present, induced the natural feeling that our boatmen were a set of rare geniuses, selected by our generous friend for the purpose of giving us additional pleasure and surprise. It was afterwards found that extemporaneous singing was not uncommon among them.

The Negro boatman of the South seems inspired by the improvising muse whenever he seizes the oar; and especially if it be to row a company of agreeable people on a party of pleasure. If there be young ladies of the number, they may be quite sure to be introduced by the muse, and to receive not only compliments, but admonitions.

Farther to pursue this subject, though it may conflict with the unity of the narrative, there may be told a brief story of a case of improvisation, on a subsequent occasion, of a very striking and characteristic nature; and by no means a bad illustration of the scope and power of the poetic muse.

At the time alluded to, there was an unmarried planter of large property in the country, whose character was not at all enviable, as either a Gentleman or a Master; although he had received an education which should have made him a model in both characters.

A party of ladies and gentlemen were passing down the river on a retiring tide, and the oarsmen had little other labor but to keep time with their oars. After a low preparatory talk among themselves, they entered upon an extemporaneous song of considerable length, and not without artistic merit. The chorus had evidently been concerted among them; for the whole united in it at the first recurrence, so as to make the shores reverberate it, and particularly the last word – the name of the victimized planter.

He was described by the leader of the music, as a rich and handsome young man, with fine house and gardens;- horses and carriages; and all desirable things for comfort and elegance. But all these advantages are represented as more than counterbalanced by bad qualities of heart and conduct, described and exemplified to excite abhorrence. And all unmarried ladies, by name, one after the other, are warned not to be tempted by his wealth and splendor to marry him; because bad masters make bad husbands.- "Don't you marry *********," The name itself was replete with melody, and its structure and vowel sounds wonderfully adapted to musical effect.

I know of no name in our language to compare with it in musical sound; and when it came back in echo to our ears from the distant shore of the broad St. Johns, the effect was wonderful. Could I give that name it would far better illustrate my meaning than I can describe it. It must not be. Long since his race of unhappy profligacy had been run; but surviving relatives of worth and excellence might be wounded by the needless reminiscence.

CHAPTER X.

DRAYTON ISLAND.

When we arrived at the beautiful island of our destination, the doctor had become nearly as joyous as the Negroes themselves. And then we had the pleasure to look on another phase of the obnoxious system of human brutalization, well adapted to deepen the favorable impression made on his perhaps too susceptible feelings.

For the purpose of propagating several rare and valuable varieties of tropical plants, from the ocean islands and other foreign regions, the proprietor of Drayton Island had placed on it a little colony of two or three families of his own household, under the deputed patriarchal oversight of the senior, and mostly, the progenitor, of the colony; a grave old man, who had been rescued many years before from the cruel tyranny of a savage African master. We landed on the shore of the island at the opposite extremity from the settlement. Hence, we rambled through the plantations and nurseries of tropical plants and trees, defended from ungenial winds by the indigenous forest, bursting into spring beauty and sweetness, and made more paradisiacal by the unrivalled bird-music of the south, mingling with the soothing murmur of the pine leaves— like "the aggregate of many gentle movements of gentle creatures"—and with the ceaseless ripple of the surrounding lake. The little birds that love the ground, hopped along before us; and gorgeously resplendent clouds of ten thousands of paroquets, sailed high over the silvery lake in such paradise of a home—a home, such as any man or woman ought to be ashamed not to be happy in.

Entranced by such varied charms, too soon, as we felt, we came to the home of the sable islanders. We had feared to find ourselves there, too rudely precipitated from the height to which our pleasurable emotions had been elevated. Our fears had been groundless. The happy condition of humanity that opened on our view was but adapted to confirm and make practical, so to say, our previous and pleasant experience. At their easy and pleasant garden work we found these happy people. They smiled upon us a kind of greeting from among the orange, lemon, and lime trees; all starred over with white blossoms, relieving most charmingly the deep ground of rich green leaves of every shade of grateful color.

From their own provision grounds, which they were planting with corn, okra, potatoes of both kinds, cassava, arrow-root, melons, and other delicious southern vegetables, they had come in to enjoy a luxurious two hours, with the late breakfast, which every southern negro best likes, and especially, as on the present occasion, when he may extend a welcome hospitality to the friendly stranger.

"Well, well," said the doctor, "this seems to me to realize an ideal of some dream, that some time or other I have had; unless, indeed, I am now dreaming!"

"You are not dreaming, doctor. This scene, and this island, and lake, and life scenery, are all real."

"I think so. And if so, living in harmony and love, as these people seem to, and in such delightful circumstances, in this genial and lovely climate, if any human condition may be happy, what can interfere with the happiness of these people?"

The above book expressed a pro slavery point of view, the abolitionists published many books that encouraged the end of slavery.

Chapter 15: Indian villages

Only a small percentage of the Indians in the new world were in Florida. I found a list of Florida Indian villages on the internet. In each of these villages there were people whose lives were profoundly affected by the colonization of Florida.

Maybe we should have a moment of silence for each village, or say a prayer.

The following list of Indian villages is included to emphasize the plight of the native peoples of North and South America. The suffering of the Indians and the Slaves during this period of history is probably being equaled today in some part of the world.

Indian Villages Florida the latter, though some of the subdivisions given should be rated as independent tribes. (See Timuqua under Georgia.)
http://freepages.genealogy.rootsweb.ancestry.com/~prsjr/na/se/fl_pg1.htm

Utina or Timuqua tribe: Towns

Laudeniere (1586) states that there were more than 40 under the Utina chief, but among them he includes "Acquera"

(Acuera) and Moquoso far to the south and entirely independent, so that we are uncertain regarding the status of the others he gives, which are as follows. Cadechn, Calnnay, Chilili, Eclauou, Molona, Omittaqua, and Onachaquara.

As the Utina, with the possible exception of the Potano, was the leading Timucua division and gave its name to the whole, and as the particular tribe to which each town mentioned in the documents belonged cannot be given, it will be well to enter all here, although those that can be placed more accurately will be inserted in their proper places.

In De Soto's time Aguacaleyquen or Caliquen seems to have been the principal town. In the mission period we are told that the chief lived at Ayaocuto.

Acassa, a town inland from Tampa Bay. Aguacaleyquen, a town in the province of Utina between Suwannee and Santa Fe Rivers. Ahoica, probably near the Santa Fe River. Alachepoyo, inland from Tampa Bay. Alatico, probably on Cumberland Island. Albino, 40 leagues or 4 days inland from St. Augustine and within 1 1/2 to 2 leagues of two others called Tucuro and Utiaca. Alimacani, on an island of the same name not far north of the mouth of St. Johns River. Amaca, inland from Tampa Bay. Anacapa, in the Fresh Water Province 20 leagues south of St. Augustine.

Anacharaqua, location unknown. Antonico, in the Fresh Water Province. Apalu, in the province of Yustaga. Arapaja, 70 leagues from St. Augustine, Probably on Alapaha River. Araya, south of the Withlacoochee River. Archaha, location unknown. Assile, on or near Aucilla River. Astina, location unknown. Atuluteca, probably near San Pedro or Cumberland Island. Ayacamale, location unknown. Ayaocute, in the Utina country 34 leagues from St. Augustine. Ayotore, inland from Cumberland Island and probably southwest.

Beca, location unknown. Becao, location unknown. Bejesi, location unknown, perhaps the Apalachee town of Wacissa. Cachipile, 70 leagues west of St. Augustine. Cacoroy, south of St. Augustine and 1 1/2 leagues from Nocoroco, probably in the Fresh Water Province.

Cadecha, allied with Utina. Calany, allied with Utina. Caparaca, south of St. Augustine, southwest of Nocoroco and probably in the Fresh Water Province. Casti, location unknown. Cayuco, near Tampa Bay. Chamini, 70 leagues west of St. Augustine. Chimaucayo, south of St. Augustine. Chinica, 70 leagues from St. Augustine. Cholupaha, south of Aguacaleyquen in the Potano Province. Chuaquin, 60 leagues west of St. Augustine. Cicale, south of St. Augustine and 3 leagues south of Nocoroco, perhaps in the Fresh Water Province. Cilili, said to be a Utina town. Colucuchia, several leagues south of Nocoroco. Coya, location unknown.

Disnica, south of St. Augustine, perhaps should be Tisnica. Ecalamototo, on the site of Picolata. Ecita, near Tampa Bay, possibly a variant of Ocita. Eclsuou, location unknown. Edelano, on an island of the same name in St. Johns River. Elajay, location unknown, perhaps Calusa. Elanogue, in the Fresh Water Province near Antonico. Emola, location unknown. Enecaque, location unknown. Equale, in the Fresh Water Province. Ereze, inland from Tampa Bay. Esquega, a town or tribe on the west coast. Exangue, near Cumberland Island.

Filache, in the Fresh Water Province. Guacara, on Suwannee River in northwestern Florida. Guacoco, probably a town on a plain so called in the Urriparacoxi country.

Heliocopile, location unknown. Helmacape, location unknown. Hicachirico ("Little town"), one league from the mission of San Juan. del Puerto, which was probably at the mouth of St. Johns River in the Saturiwa Province. Hiocaia, the probable name of a town giving its name to a chief, location unknown. Huara, inland from Cumberland Island.

Itaraholata, south of Potano, Potano Province. Juraya, a rancheria, apparently in the Timucua territory. Laca, another name for Ecalamototo.

Lamale, inland from Cumberland Island. Luca, between Tampa Bay and the Withlacoochee River in the Urriparacoxi country.

Machaba, 64 leagues from St. Augustine, near the northern border of the Timucua country inland. Maiaca, the town of the Fresh Water Province most distant from St. Augustine, a few leagues north of Cape Canaveral and on St. Johns River. Malaca, south of Nocoroco. Marracou, location unknown. Mathiaqua, location unknown. Mayajuaca, near Maiaca. Mayaru, on lower St. Johns River. Mocama, possibly a town on Cumberland Island, province of Tacatacuru, but probably a province. Mogote, south of St. Augustine in the region of Nocoroco. Moloa, on the south side of St. Johns River near its mouth, province of Saturiwa.

Napa, on an island one league from Cumberland Island. Napituca, north of Aguacaleyquen, province of Utina. Natobo, a mission station and probably native town 2 1/2 leagues from San Juan del Puerto at the mouth of St. Johns River, province of Saturiwa. Nocoroeo, at the mouth of a river, perhaps Halifax River, one day's journey south of Matanzas Inlet, Fresh Water Province.

-

Ocale, in a province of the same name in the neighborhood of the present Ocala. Ocita, probably on Terra Ceia Island, on Hillsborough Bay. Onathaqua, a town or tribe near Cape Canaveral. Osigubede, a chief and probably town on the west coast. Panara, inland from Cumberland Island. Parca, location unknown. Patica, on the seacoast 8 leagues south of the mouth of St. Johns River. Pebe, a chief and probably a town on the west coast. Pentoaya, at the head of Indian River. Perquymaland, south of Nocoroco; possibly the names of two towns, Perqui and Maland, run together.

Pia, on the east coast south of Nocoroco. Pitano, a mission station and probably a native town a league and a half from Puturiba. Pohoy, a town or province, or both, at Tampa Bay, and perhaps a synonym of Ocita. Potano, the principal town of the Potano tribe, on the Alachua plains. Potaya, 4 leagues from San Juan del Puerto at the mouth of St. Johns River. Puala, near Cumberland Island. Punhuri, inland from Cumberland Island. Puturiba, probably near the northern end of Cumberland Island, province of Tacatacuru. There was another town of the same name west of the Suwannee River.

Sabobche, near the coast south of Nocoroco. Saint Julian, in the Fresh Water Province. San Mateo, about 2 leagues from San

Juan del Puerto at the mouth of St. Johns River, province of Saturiwa. San Pablo, about 1 1/2 leagues from San Juan del Puerto, province of Saturiwa. San Sebastian, on an arm of the sea near St. Augustine. Sarauahi, a quarter of a league from San Juan del Puerto. Sena, on an "inlet" north of the mouth of St. Johns River, perhaps Amelia River. Siyagueche, near Cape Canaveral. Socochuno, location unknown. Soloy, not far from St. Augustine and probably on the river called Seloy by the French. Surruque, a town or tribe near Cape Canaveral.

Tacatacuru, the name of Cumberland Island and Province, and perhaps of the chief town, on the mainland side of the island near the southern end, 2 leagues from the Barra de San Pedro.

Tafocole, inland from Tampa Bay. Tahupa, inland from Cumberland Island. Tanpacaste, a chief and perhaps town north of Pohoy, i. e., north of Tampa Bay. Tarihica, 54 leagues from St. Augustine, and perhaps in the Onatheaqua Province. Tocaste, on a large lake south of the Withlacoochee River, province of Urriparacoxi. Tocoaya, very near Cumberland Island. Tocobaga, the chief town of the province so called, in Safety Harbor, Tampa Bay. Tocoy, in the Fresh Water Province 5 leagues south of St. Augustine. Tolapatafi, probably toward the west coast of the peninsula of Florida near Aucilla River. Toloco, location unknown.

Tomeo, near the Fresh Water Province. Tucura, near the Fresh Water Province. Tucuro, see Abino. Tunsa, possibly a synonym of Antonico.

Ucachile, a town or tribe in the Yustaga Province, perhaps the mother town of the Osochi. Uqueten, the southernmost village of the province of Ocale on Withlacoochee River entered by De Soto. Urica, 60 leagues from St. Augustine. Uriutina, just north of the river of Aguacaleyquen, perhaps at Lake City. Urubia, near Cape Canaveral and 1 1/2 leagues from the town of Surruque.

Utayne, inland from Cumberland Island. Utiaca, see Abino.

Utichini, inland from Cumberland Island and within a league and a half of Puturiba. Utinamocharra, 1 day's journey north of Poiano, Potano Province. Vera Cruz, half a league from San Juan del Puerto, province of Saturiwa. Vicela, a short distance south of Withlacoochee River, province of uraracoxi. Xapuica, near the Guale country, perhaps a synonym of Caparaca.

Xatalalnno, inland from Cumberland Island. Yaocay, near Antonico in the Fresh Water Province. Yeapalano, inland from Cumberland Island and probably within half a league or a league of Puturiba. Yufera, inland and probably northwest from Cumberland Island.

Calusa tribe: Villages

In the following list the letters (S) and (I) indicate respectively towns belonging to the (S)eacoast Division and those of the (I)nterior Division about Lake Okeechobee Beyond this allocation the positions of most of the towns may be indicated merely in a general manner, by reference to neighboring towns.

Abir (I), between Neguitun and Cutespa. Alcola (or Chosa), location uncertain. Apojola Negra, the first word is Timucua; the second seems to be Spanish; location unknown. Calaobe (S). Caragara, between Namuguya and Henhenguepa. Casitoa (S), between Muspa and Cotebo. Cayovea (S). Cayucar, between Tonco and Neguitun. Chipi, between Tomcobe and Taguagemae. Chosa (see Alcola). Comachica (S). Cononoguay, between Cutespa and Estegue. Cotebo, between Casitoa and Coyobia. Coyobia, between Cotebo and Tequemapo. Cuchiyaga, said to be southwest from Bahia Honda and 40 leagues northeast of Guarungube, probably on Big Pine Key. Custavui, south of Jutun. Cutespa (I), between Abir and Cononoguay. Elafay, location uncertain. Enempa (I). Estame (S), between Metamapo and Sacaspada. Estantapaca, between Yagua and Queyhicha. Estegue, between Cononoguay and Tomsobe. Excuru, between Janar and Metamapo. Guarungube, "on the point of the Martyrs," and thus probably near Key West.

Guevu (S). Henhenguepa, between Caragara and Ocapataga. Janar, between Ocapataga and Escuru. Judyi, between Satucuava and Soco. Juestocobaga, between Queyhicha and Sinapa. Jutun (S), between Tequemapo and Custavui. Metamapo (S), between Escuru and Estame. Muspa (S), between Teyo and Casitoa. Numuguya, between Taguagemae and Caragara. Neguitun, between Cayucar and Abir. No or Non (S).Ocapataga, between Henhenguepa and Janar. Queyhicha, between Estantapaca and Juestocobaga. Quisiyove (S). Sacaspada (S), between Estame and Satucuava. Satucuava, between Sacaspada and Judyi. Sinaesta (S). Sinapa (S), between Juestocobaga and Tonco. Soco, between Judyi and Vuebe. Taguagemae, between Chipi and Namuguya. Tampa (S), the northernmost town, followed on the south by Yegua, and probably on Charlotte Harbor. Tatesta (S), between the Tequesta tribe and Cuchiyaga, about 80 leagues north of the latter, perhaps at the innermost end of the Keys. Tavaguemue (I). Tequemapo (S), between Goyobia and Jutun. Teyo, between Vuebe and Muspa. Tiquijagua (?). Tomo (S).Tomsobe (I), between Estegue and Chipi. Tonco, between Sinapa and Cayucar. **Tuchi (S).** Vuebe, between Soco and Teyo, possibly the same as Guevu. Yagua (S), between Tampa and Estantapaca.

Seminole tribe: Villages Ahnpopka, near the head of Ocklawaha River. Ahosulga, 5 miles south of New Mikasuki, perhaps in Jefferson County. Alachua, near Ledwiths Lake. Alafiers, probably a synonym for some other town name, perhaps McQueen's Village, near Alafia River. Alapaha, probably on the west side of the Suwannee just above its junction with the Allapaha. Alligator, said to be a settlement in Suwannee County. Alouko, on the east side of St. Marks River 20 miles north of St. Marks. Apukasasoche, 20 miles west of the head of St. Johns River. Attapulgas first Iwation, west of Apalachicola River in Jackson or Calhoun Counties; second location inland in Gadsden County. Beech Creek, exact location unknown. Big Cypress Swamp, in the "Devil's Garden" on the northern edge of Big Cypress Swamp, 15 to 20 miles southwest of Lake Okeechobee. Big Hammock, north of Tampa Bay.

Bowlegs' Town, chief's name, on Suwannee River and probably known usually under another name. Bucker Woman's Town, on Long Swamp east of Big Hammocok. Burges' Town, probably on or near Flint or St. Marys River, southwestern Georgia. Calusahatchee, on the river of the same name and probably occupied by Calusa Indians. Capola, east of St. Marks River. Catfish Lake, on a small lake in Polk County nearly midway between Lake Pierce and Lake Rosalie, toward the headwaters of Kissimmee River. Chefixico's Old Town, on the south side of Old Tallahassee Lake, 5 miles east of Tallahassee. Chetuckota, on the west bank of Pease Creek, below Pease Lake, west central Florida. Choconikla, on the west side of Apalachicola River, probably in Jackson County. Chohalaboohulka, probably identical with Alapaha. Chukochati, near the hammock of the same name. Cohowofooche, 23 miles northwest of St. Marks. Cow Creek, on a stream about 15 miles northeast of the entrance of Kissimmee River. Cuscowilla (see Alachua).

Etanie, west of St. Johns River and east of Black Creek. Etotulga, 10 miles east of Old Mikasuki. Fish-eating Creek, F, miles from a creek emptying into Lake Okeechobee. Fulemmy's Town, perhaps identical with Beech Creek, Suwannee River. Elatchcalamocha, near Drum Swamp, 18 miles west of New Mikasuki. Hiamonee, on the east bank of Ockiocknee River, probably on Lake Iamonia. Hitchapuksassi, about 20 miles from the head of Tampa Bay and 20 miles south-east of Chukochati.

Homosassa, probably on Homosassa River. Iolee, 60 miles above the mouth of Apalachicola River on the west bank at or near Blountstown. John Hicks' Town, west of Payne's Savannah. King Heijah's Town, or Koe Hadjo's Town, consisted of Negro slaves, probably in Alachua County. Lochchiocha, 60 miles east of Apalaohicola River and near Ocklocknee **River.**

Loksachumpa, at the head of St. Johns River. Lowwalta (probably for Liwahali), location unknown. McQueen's Village, on the east side of Tampa Bay, perhaps identical with Alafiers. Miami River, about 10 miles north of the site of Fort Dallas, not far from Biscayne Bay, on Little Miami River. Mulatto Girl's Town, south of Tuscawilla Lake. Negro Town, near Withlacoochee River, probably occupied largely by runaway slaves. New Mikasuki, 30 miles west of Suwannee River, probably in Madison County. Notasulgar, location unknown.Ochisi, at a bluff so called on the east side of Apalachicola River. Ochupocrassa, near Miami.

Ocilla, at the mouth of Aucilla River on the east side. Oclackonayahe, above Tampa Bay. Oclawaha, on Ocklawaha River, probably in Putnam County. Oithlakutci, on Little River 40 miles east of Apalachicola River. Okehumpkee, 60 miles southwest from Volusia. Oktahatki, 7 miles northeast of Sampala. Old Mikasuki, near Miccosukee in Leon County. Oponays, "back of Tampa Bay," probably in Hillsboro or Polk Counties. Owassissas, on an eastern branch of St. Marks River and probably near its head. Payne's Town, near Koe Hadjo's Town, occupied by Negroes. Picolata, on the east bank of St. Johns River west of St. Augustine. Pilaklikaha, about 120 miles south of Alachua. Pilatka, on or near the site of Palatka, probably the site of a Seminole town and of an earlier town as well. Red Town, at Tampa Bay. **Sampala, 26 miles above the forks of the Apalachicola on the west** bank, in Jackson County, or in Houston County, Ala. Santa Fe, on the river of the same name, perhaps identical with Washitokha. Sarasota, at or near Sarasota. Seleuxa, at the head of Aucilla River. Sitarky, evidently named after a chief, between Camp Izard and Fort King, West Florida. Spanawalka, a miles below Iolee and on the west bank of Apalaehicola River. Suwannee, on the west bank of Suwannee River in Lafayette County. Talakhacha, on the west side of Cape Florida on the seacoast. Tallahassee, on the site of present Tallahassee. Tallahassee or Spring Gardens, 10 miles from Volusia, occupied by Yuchi. Talofa Okhase, about 30 miles west southwest from the upper part of Lake George. Taluschapkoapopka, a short distance west of upper St. Johns River, probably at the present Apopka. Tocktoethla, 10 miles above the junction of Chattahoochee and Flint Rivers. Tohopki lagi, probably near Miami. Topananaulka, 3 miles west of New Mikasuki. Topkegalga, on the east side of Ocklocknee River near Tallahassee. Totstalahoeetska, on the west side of Tampa Bay.

Tuckagulga, on the east side of Ocklocknee River between it and Hiamonee. Tuslalahockaka, 10 miles west of Walalecooche. Wacahoota, location unknown. Wachitokha, on the east side of Suwannee River between Suwannee and Santa Fe Rivers. Wakasassa, on the coast east of the mouth of Suwannee River. Wasupa, 2 miles from St. Marks River and 18 miles from St. Marks itself. Wechotookme, location unknown. Weliks, 4 miles east of the Tallahassee town. Wewoka, at Wewoka, Okla. Willanoucha, at the head of St. Marks River, perhaps identical with Alouko. Withlacoochee, on Withlacoochee River, probably in Citrus or Sumter County. Withlako, 4 miles from Clinch's battle ground. Yalacasooche, at the mouth of Ocklawaha River. Yulaka, on the west side of St. Johns River, 35 miles from Volusia or Dexter. Yumersee, at the head of St. Marks River, 2 miles north of St. Marks, a settlement of Yamasee. (See Georgia.)

Authors Note:: The above ends the list of Indian villages in Florida

The island Utina or Timuqua village of Edelano is now Drayton island. It is clear that many Indians lived in Florida when the Europeans arrived. The rest of North and South America were similarly populated by Indians. Some estimate a total of twenty five million Indians lived in the new world when the Europeans arrived.

Chapter 16 Working Plantation

In 1965 my brother and I started looking for a farm to buy in the Hudson Valley of New York. We found a farm that fit our feet and an owner who was ready to quit. We bought it with a promise down and great expectations. The joke going around at that time was as follows: Governor Cuomo asked a new lottery winner: Well farmer Brown what are you going to do now that you have all of this money? Farmer Brown scratched his head and said, well governor, I guess I will just keep farming until it is all gone. Another: Two assets a farmer needs are a good education and a wife that drives a school bus.

We lasted 23 years until our money was all gone then sold it for development. The point I am making is that it is not easy to operate a profitable farm. The lessons learned this year cannot be used until next year. If you think that in eight years the consumer will be buying red apples, when your red apple orchard begins full production in eight years they will be buying yellow or green apples or maybe tomatillos.

There are lots of people that do not know about farming because it has become a capital intensive business rather than a labor intensive business. In the early days of Florida development the farming was based upon the hand labor of men and women working in the hot Florida sun.

Arriving in Florida before the mid 1800's a settler was faced with attacking the jungle with hand tools. (NO they did not have chain saws and D-8 bulldozers) The good land that would be good for raising crops is already busy growing a mixture of plants of all descriptions. The first thing to do would be to cut down a big tree as a good start. This first tree may decide to lean on its neighbor tree and hang there waiting for you to cut the neighboring tree and then fall on you. Pulling two more down on top because of the intertwining vines.

If you outwit the trees that want to fall on you, you will have a lot of logs and branches on the ground that have to be moved to the place of burning. I guess that an acre of big trees might have four hundred trees that weigh about one thousand pounds each. That amounts to about 200 tons of stuff on each acre. Even if you have a strong kid to help you, that's a lot of work. If you burn that much wood, the ashes may affect the soil for several years.

Now you are faced with grubbing out the smaller plants around the big tree stumps. The soil that you are planning to use is already full of roots; there are more roots than soil. Some of these roots are thicker than your wrists and as long as they want to be.

In those days, if you had a horse or mule or a pair of oxen they would be a big help in clearing the land. Even with good animals and plows and harrows it will be four or five years before you get rid of all of the stumps and have a decent field ready for crops. In the meantime you can plant around the obstructions like stumps and get a part crop.

Hidden in the woods around your new field there are animals that look forward to you planting and raising a crop of food, food that they will eat before you get to harvest it. Hidden under your feet and all around you are insects and other organisms that will also enjoy the new crops that you are planting. Hidden, but ready to spring into action are seeds and parts of plants that will compete with, and probably defeat, the crop you are planting.

Additionally, the rain falls too much in some months and not enough in other months. Periodic winter freezes kill all of the tender plants. Indians attack and steal your animals and tools. The great powers of the world reshuffle the deck and you no longer own your land. No-one said it would be easy.

The essence of farming is to destroy all plants, animals, insects and diseases that injure your crop and to provide soil conditions, water and nutrients that nature fails to provide. It is a war. It is not easy. It is hard work in the hot sun. Much must be put in before anything comes out.

It must have been a tremendous problem to organize slaves and other workers to successfully raise a good profitable crop. Brute force would not work because it would be easy for workers to do small things that would defeat your purpose. Overseers had to be diplomats to make it work. It was no Sunday picnic.

One of the most important export crops during the British period 1763-1784, cotton is a fiber that grows in a boll around the seeds of the cotton plant. The plant is a shrub native to tropical and subtropical regions around the world. It is planted in early spring and harvested in the fall and winter.

Cotton was grown in Mexico eight thousand years ago. Prior to the invention of machinery, the growing and harvesting of cotton required a great deal of hand labor. The invention of the improved cotton gin in 1795 and the spinning and weaving machinery of the industrial revolution demanded more cotton.

The demand for cotton was transformed into a demand for slaves on the plantations of the south. In 1830 the south exported 720,000 bales of cotton. Thirty years later in 1860, the south exported seven times as much!

They exported five million bales of cotton. It is hard to imagine how many slave work days it took to raise and harvest five million bales of cotton in one year. Prior to the American Revolution the American colonies relied upon cotton and other exports to make financing the revolution possible. The slaves made the revolution possible.

All of the work, clearing the land, preparing the fields, planting and caring for the crop, harvesting the crop, processing the cotton and financing all of the above had to be planned and carried out by businessmen with capital or good credit. The work was done by slaves who had no say in the matter but were as important as any other factor.

Turpentine and naval stores were the second most important export during the British period 1763-1784. Originally naval stores referred to resin-based components used in building and maintaining ships. This included turpentine, rosin, pitch (resin) and tar. These products were produced by scarring the bark of a pine tree and collecting and processing the sap that oozes out of the tree at the cut made by the bark hack tool. The hack produces an 8 inch long and one inch wide gouge through the cambium layer of the tree and a piece of galvanized metal is installed to direct the sap into a one quart cup attached to the tree. Multiple successive cuts scar the trees up to seven feet high.

Millions of naturally occurring pine trees were visited by slaves and millions of quarts of sap were brought into the central camp to be distilled and barreled up for export. Harvesting continued until the 1920's when a lack of labor and the availability of other products from the petroleum industry made the practice unprofitable.

Corn: An important provision crop required to support the people living on the plantation. Corn is planted as a seed in rows or hills. The plants must be kept free of competing weeds until they become large enough to shade out the weeds. The corn stalks produce ears that are harvested and dried. Dried corn will keep for a year or more. Corn is important as a livestock feed and for human consumption. Most animals love corn and will steal it before it is harvested.

Rice: An important export crop during the British Period 1763-1784. Rice is planted in a field that can be flooded and drained as required to maintain irrigation to the thirsty rice plants and to flood the base of the plant killing the weeds. The water control system included an impound lake as a source of fresh water and a drainage system to remove the field water when desired. Dams, gates, canals, and a terrain that provides a natural slope are required for the removal of the water. Some pumps were used. Two crops of rice were possible each year in northeast Florida. During the last part of the growing season when the rice kernels fill out the field is kept full of water to help hold the rice upright.

The harvest requires the rice plant to be cut with a sickle and dried. The dry rice is then threshed to remove the rice from the straw. The rice was then separated from the chaff. The cleaned rice was pounded to remove the husks and cuticles. The finished rice was shipped in barrels that were made on the plantation. The slaves brought rice growing knowledge with them from Africa.

Tobacco is seeded into a hot bed or cold frame to prevent attacks by insects in the spring of the year. When the plants are established they are transplanted into the field. Tobacco requires great attention to detail to produce a good quality crop. Harvested tobacco is cured on the farm by air drying or fire drying. There are many varieties of tobacco plants. In general, tobacco requires skillful, experienced growers to produce a fine crop.

Indigo: Another important export crop during the British period 1763 to 1784. Indigo is a plant that may produce three cuttings a year in May, July and October. The plant stems and leaves are soaked in lime water and fermented for 12 to 18 hours that culminated in a blue froth. The frothy liquid was put in a beater tank and oxygen was beat into the solution with paddles. At the proper time lye was added and a precipitate was formed that sunk to the bottom of the vat. The precipitate was dried into bricks and packed in barrels and exported for use as a textile dye. Indigo dye is the dye of blue jeans. Large quantities of Indigo dye was grown and processed in India. In the 1890's it was synthesized and the growing of Indigo is not as important today as it once was.

Oranges: Oranges and other citrus fruit varieties are produced on trees that grow from the seeds found in the citrus fruit. Common sour oranges can become wild and be found anywhere the climate and growing conditions permit. Freezing temperatures will kill the trees. There are many varieties of oranges that are desirable. These desirable varieties are budded onto tree root stocks that have good growing characteristics. The orange tree can grow 20 feet high and produce nearly a ton of oranges in a good season. The trees have green leaves year around, they blossom in March and the fruit is ready from

November to February. Fresh fruit and barrels of orange juice were sold for export. A tree begins to produce enough fruit to cover expenses in about five years from planting. Deer love orange trees.

Cattle: Cattle were raised for the production of milk and dairy products, meat such as beef and veal and for use as draft animals. Milk cows were kept on the plantation because they required daily milking and special care. Meat cattle were let run on the range and rounded up from time to time to cut the steers and to sell the excess cattle. Draft animals such as oxen are large breeds. Often they are castrated males trained to respond to commands: get up, whoa, back up, gee, haw (R&L). Oxen were used in plowing, transport, hauling, and logging. Oxen can pull harder and longer than horses but they are not as fast. Slaves were raised and trained to care for the animals and to work with the animals.

Seminole Indians controlled vast areas in interior Florida and ran cattle on the grasslands. The Indians supplied beef to the Confederacy before, during and after the Civil war. The open range existed in Florida for many years after the invention of barbed wire in 1867.

Horses: The Spanish brought the first horses to Florida. The Indians had never seen a horse and the sight of a Spanish soldier dressed in armor seated on an armored horse with a sword or fire spitting gun was a wonder. After 1560 horses were common and used to ride, pull wagons and farm implements.

Mules: A mule is a hybrid equid, a cross of a female horse and a male donkey. They were used to pull farm implements and can do many of the tasks of a horse. Many operators prefer a mule to a horse because they have more patience and endurance. Mules are highly intelligent.

Hogs: Hog Island, the island next to Drayton Island is largely wetlands and was used as an open range for pigs. Pigs will eat anything but will survive on leaves, grass, roots, fruits and flowers. Hernando Desoto brought the first pigs to Florida. The female pig will begin breeding at 8-18 months and a litter of piglets contains 6-12 piglets. Pigs have no sweat glands and cool themselves in water and mud. The mud protects them from sunlight and insects. Pigs root up and dig in the earth and they cannot be allowed where crops are grown.

Fish: On a large plantation near a fishery, one or more slaves were permanently assigned to fish to supply the entire plantation with whatever seafood was available. These fishermen were chosen for their natural ability to catch fish. They used every method available

Carpenter: A large plantation would have a carpenter shop with one or more skilled slaves. The tools would be cared for by the blacksmith and the carpenter. Many projects such as building buildings, maintaining wagons & boats, making harness, hand tools and the cooperage of shipping barrels and boxes would be shared by the blacksmith and the carpenter.

Blacksmith: A blacksmith worked with metals, primarily iron creating tools, agricultural implements, cooking utensils, horseshoes and weapons. They work with iron by heating the metal in a fire of burning coal, coke or charcoal. The blacksmith controls the shape of the fire and the amount of air forced into the fire. The hot iron is shaped by hammering it on an anvil using specialized tools. Iron has been produced for more than a thousand years. Bog iron, found in some swamps, or iron ore is mixed with charcoal and burned in a furnace at temperatures as high as 2400 degrees obtained by forcing air into the furnace.

Without any machinery, several men working together over a period of twelve hours can produce several pounds of iron suitable for use by a blacksmith. Bog iron, found in streams, charcoal from the pinelands and oyster shells were combined in New Jersey furnaces to produce iron for a century beginning in 1760. In Massachusetts iron making began in 1652. This iron was sold throughout the colonies.

Salt manufacturing in Florida produced salt from sea water in solar ponds and by wood fired evaporation. Poor people with little or no capital could produce salt. Salt was a vital preservative used by food processors in the age of no refrigeration.

Smoking Meats: Every plantation had a smoke house to preserve the excess meat of animals killed for food. A combination of slow, low temperature cooking and dehydration extended the time that meat could be kept without severe deterioration. When a large animal was killed for food, skilled people would divide the carcass and some parts would be eaten immediately, some would be smoked, some parts would be pickled or salted down in barrels. Neighboring plantations would trade fresh meat for corn or other staples.

Making moonshine, homemade whiskey, wine or other alcoholic beverages was another way of preserving perishable fruits or grain into something of value that could be stored for long periods and sold or traded for other goods.00

A sawmill that prepared local trees for use as lumber or timbers for handles, furniture, buildings, docks, breakwaters, fences and other uses was a useful addition to a plantation. The carpenters used wood from the sawmill and iron from the blacksmith shop to make many of the tools and implements used on the plantation.

Chapter 17 Places to look 04-26-2013
When you have the time and the interest:

http://en.wikipedia.org/wiki/Colonial_history_of_the_United_States

-

http://www.drbronsontours.com/bronsonhistorypageamericanstaugustinecivilwar.html

http://fcit.usf.edu/Florida/lessons/cvl_war/cvl_war1.htm

http://docsouth.unc.edu/neh/wheatley/menu.html

http://www.civilwarhome.com/navalwar.htm

http://trailgatorart.blogspot.com/

http://memory.loc.gov/cgi-bin/ampage?collId=mesn&fileName=023/mesn023.db&recNum=58&itemLink=D%3Fmesnbib%3A1%3A.%

http://www.unf.edu/floridahistoryonline/Plantations/

http://www.lowcountryafricana.com/william-drayton-b.-1732.asp

http://www.astorflorida.com/history.htm

http://freepages.genealogy.rootsweb.ancestry.com/~prsjr/na/se/fl_pg1.htm

http://volusiahistory.com/howthey.htm

http://books.google.com/books?id=3ak0AAAAMAAJ&pg=RA1-PA231&dq=drayton+island+florida&hl=en&ei=ajo-TbLaEIHEgAfzx8T

http://books.google.com/books?id=ZBkkzie_DYMC&pg=PA440&lpg=PA440&dq=1855+Anzie+island+auctioned+to+duff+green&source=bl&ots=1Xeeyl_qG-&sig=LcKcrpqNPZtx6VqpcecpYUYlSYI&hl=en&sa=X&ei=U0lRT8GOHM

-

Th0QH7qYDtDQ&sqi=2&ved=0CB8Q6AEwAA#v=onepage&q=1855%20Anzie%20island%20auctioned%20to%20duff%20green&f=false

http://www.cowanauctions.com/auctions/item.aspx?ItemId=80928

http://web.archive.org/web/20091027101439/http://geocities.com/fcphs/Horse_Landing_Project.html

http://ehistory.osu.edu/uscw/features/battles/states/florida/0001.cfm

http://www.unf.edu/floridahistoryonline//Plantations/plantations/

Made in the USA
Middletown, DE
24 January 2022